I0553816

Billionaire

Auction

Billionaire Club Series

By Tia Fanning and
Brynn Paulin

Supernova Indie

Publishing Services, LLC

www.supernovaindie.com
Powered by Your Imagination

Billionaire Auction
by
Tia Fanning and Brynn Paulin

He has a paddle. Maybe he'll bid…

After her father is caught embezzling millions, Moriah agrees to sell herself in a Billionaire's Auction – one weekend and her virginity awarded to the highest bidder. While she might appear as the doting daughter, doing whatever is necessary to keep her father out of prison, Moriah has much more at stake than securing the freedom of a parent she despises. She'll do whatever she has to do to keep her sister safe.

Her first time should be for love, not for sacrifice…

When Kendrick gave Moriah's father three days to return the stolen money, he never imagined the scoundrel would set up some twisted "virginity auction" and sell his daughter to one of their perverted billionaire clients. Kendrick will be damned if he'll let that Moriah prostitute herself for her greedy father. It's not going to happen. Not if he can help it. And being a billionaire himself, he intends to make sure it doesn't.

Copyright © 2018,

Tia Fanning and Brynn Paulin

Billionaire Auction
Cover Art by Supernova Indie Publishing
Services, LLC
Edited by Liza Green

Electronic Format ISBN: 978-1-62344-127-2

Print Format ISBN: 978-1-62344-135-7

Published by: Supernova Indie Publishing
Services, LLC

Warning: All rights reserved. The unauthorized
reproduction or distribution of this copyrighted
work is illegal. Criminal copyright infringement,
including infringement without monetary gain, is
investigated by the FBI and is punishable by up to
5 years in federal prison and a fine of $250,000.

This is a work of fiction. Names, characters,
places and occurrences are a product of the
author's imagination. Any resemblance to actual
persons, living or dead, places or occurrences, is
purely coincidental.

Thank you for your purchase of Billionaire Auction by Tia Fanning and Brynn Paulin. We hope you've enjoyed the story and will consider leaving a review.

We love hearing from readers! Please visit our websites at <http://tiafanning.com/> and <https://www.brynnpaulin.com/>.

To all our readers. Thank you!

Chapter One

Kendrick Bergana rubbed the tension out of the back of his neck. He had to do something with his palm. Otherwise, he might pull her scantily clad rear off the platform and spank the panties right off. How dare she…how dare she do this for her father?

He locked his jaw. Ultimately, he bore some of the blame for this mess. Moriah Cabraro had vowed she would pay him back every cent her father had embezzled from his firm.

But not like this. Not auctioning herself to the highest bidder. Not sweet, innocent Moriah. He had agreed to wait three days for the money, but that was for her father to honor, not her.

And damn her father for setting up this event, for allowing his daughter to sell her virginity to keep his own sorry ass out of prison. The moment Kendrick had learned of the theft, he should have called his lawyers and been done with it. But no, he'd confronted Jof instead while his daughter had been visiting him in his office. As threats were made, Moriah had cried — literally fallen to his feet and begged him not to have her father arrested.

Kendrick looked around in disgust. He had never attended an auction like this before. Of course, he also considered himself a fairly decent human being. He avoided events that allowed people in a position of financial power to take advantage of those who weren't in such a position. No, he rather take money and assets from other billionaires, not desperate men and women needing money so badly they were willing to sell their virginity to one of these pricks.

As far as bidders were concerned, from those he recognized, her father had chosen well. These were some of Kendrick's richest clients — and some of the most depraved men on God's green earth. Men with too much money and too much time on their hands, and very little respect for women, much less sacrificial virgins willing to endure their lecherous passions for the right price. And many of these men would get their pound of flesh from her if they won the right to it.

There were at least twenty bidders, along with their assorted consorts. It looked like any other classy evening gathering he'd ever attended with his international clients at some remote mansion on someone's private island. Only, it wasn't. These men, and possibly even some of the women in attendance, were there to purchase a sordid weekend with Moriah, a certified "by three doctors" virgin.

Moriah stood tall like a regal queen, her nipples jutting through delicate white fabric. Her full breasts swept seductively under the thin, silky material whenever she moved. The plunging silk charmeuse gown showcased a slit so high that the part reached the curve of her hip, offering tantalizing glimpses of her matching panties. Diamonds sparkled around her neck and left wrist. Her dark chocolate hair, which she usually kept haphazardly in a messy bun or swept back in a ponytail, cascaded down her back in large, shiny tendrils against smooth skin like molten ganache.

Moriah was gorgeous. He always thought her beautiful, but her father had obviously insisted she dress up for the auction. Kendrick couldn't imagine her wearing something so revealing of her own accord.

He'd known her since she was a teenager — met her when his father joined the firm. Usually, she was away at private school, a devout Catholic if he remembered correctly. He almost wished that were not the case. She might not be standing up there if she were sexually experienced like most women in their twenties. He figured she must have been saving herself for the man she'd marry and start a family with. Now, her desire to give her virginity to someone she loved would be wasted on some stranger as a sacrifice for her piece of shit father.

Honor thy father and thy mother, so the Bible read.

Jofre didn't deserve to have such a loyal daughter. She was kind. She was patient. She was humble. Moriah was actually everything Jof was not.

"She must have taken after her mother," Kendrick muttered under his breath then took of swig of whisky. "God rest her soul." Anna had died from cancer a few years ago.

Kendrick was glad Anna wasn't here to see this — or rather, he wished Moriah's mother were still alive. She never would have allowed this to happen.

Jof, in his tuxedo, stood among a group of men in the parlor, laughing boisterously as if he weren't about to sell his daughter's purity to cover his debts.

At that moment, their eyes met. They hadn't seen or spoken to each other since the confrontation. *"Three days,"* Kendrick had said before he'd stormed out of the office, ordering security to escort Jof off premises as he went down the hall. It had been late. After office hours. Jof had been spared the public humiliation, and instead transferred the burden of shame to his daughter.

Kendrick wondered what Jof told the auction attendees. Jof was a wealthy man in his own right—more so for having stolen money from the firm. But what reason could he give for offering up his innocent child as a virgin sacrifice?

Regardless of the excuse, it was obviously acceptable enough to bring in a crowd. Not that people like this cared much for reasons if it suited their own desires.

Jof excused himself from the parlor conversation and ventured over. Again, Kendrick's hand itched to strike something. But rather than the flat of his palm on a firm rear, he wanted to connect his hard fist into the weak jaw of an unscrupulous jerkoff.

"I'm surprised to see you here."

I bet you are.

After all, Kendrick hadn't received an invite to this twisted soiree. When an overseas client had mentioned it offhand yesterday, he hadn't even believed it. When he was able to get confirmation that this auction was really happening, Kendrick had made arrangements of a monetary type to guarantee he'd be allowed in under someone else's invitation. He'd even managed to secure himself a bidding paddle upon arrival, which required his consent to an immediate on-the-spot blood draw. According to the contract he'd signed to participate in the auction, failure to pass the medical check negated the weekend's fun. The winner would be out of a lot of money for nothing.

When Kendrick said nothing, Jof eyed the numbered paddle. "You plan to bid on your own cow?"

The fragile whisky glass broke in Kendrick's grip even as his bloody hand snatched the bastard by his white dress shirt. "I ought to kill you myself, right here, for the piece of shit you are. Don't you dare insinuate Moriah is up there because of me."

Kendrick released his grip as the crowd's attention diverted to both of them. Men with obviously concealed weapons moved closer. Jof held them off with a lift of his hand. It popped into Kendrick's mind that he should reveal to everyone exactly what had transpired to lead to this night's auction, but one look at Moriah had him biting his tongue. Her eyes were glossy bright under the chandelier's light as if she might burst into tears at any moment. He wouldn't humiliate her more.

Rather than expose her father for the scoundrel he was, Kendrick snagged a passing waiter's towel and wrapped his injured hand. "The three-day grace period I agreed to was meant for *you* to return the money on behalf of your pleading daughter, not for you to sell her off to the highest bidder," he bit out.

"Look, Ken, I didn't steal—"

"Do not."

"You're overacting—"

Kendrick turned and walked away. If he didn't, he might truly commit the murder he'd threatened moments earlier.

Determined to end this now, he strode over to where Moriah was on display, people parting before him like the Red Sea. "Excuse me," he growled as two older men perused Moriah as if she were merchandise. "I need a moment with the lady."

The men look ready to object but then noticed the blood-soaked linen wrapped around his hand. With a nod, they left.

"Moriah," he said.

"Mr. Bergana."

"Don't do this."

"I have to," she whispered.

"No, you don't. You can walk away right now."

Her eyes welled. "No. I can't. I agreed. I signed papers—"

"It doesn't matter." Kendrick held out his hand to help her down.

"Moriah, dear, is Kendrick bothering you?" Jof, having already changed his bloody shirt, slithered up beside them. His expression said he was a concerned parent, but Kendrick knew him for the snake he was. "Or do you simply need something? Would you like some wine? Or something to relax you?" He waved over to the assortment of recreational drugs spread on a nearby coffee table where a group of younger men and women seemed to be partaking.

Lowering her lashes, she shook her head. "No, Daddy, I'm fine."

"Well, then we should begin the auction momentarily. Ken, would you like to stay and bid?" He held out his arm to indicate some open seating across the room. "Or should I have the staff escort you out to…?" Jof smiled thinly. "How did you get here again?"

By staff, Jof meant the many bodyguards who were employed by the homeowners, and the large security detail that had arrived with the guests. This was a billionaire club, though not one he was normally part of. Here, like in his personal circle, everyone had enemies, and everyone had protection. Unlike with his more upstanding colleagues, everyone in attendance at this auction would side with Jof if they wanted to have a chance at winning Moriah. Kendrick would have no allies.

"I'm here to bid," he assured quietly.

Chapter Two

Moriah couldn't believe that Kendrick was there. Heat flushed over her face and down to her toes. It took everything in her not to flee the mirrored platform.

She'd had a crush on Kendrick from the first time she'd seen him, some seven years ago when she'd been fourteen. He'd seen her in some of the most awkward stages of her life, and now, he was there to witness the most humiliating.

Too embarrassed to actually look at him, she watched him stalk away, anger clearly vibrating from his tall, powerful frame. Dark haired with piercing silvery-blue eyes, he shone among the lesser men here. Oh sure, the vultures were rich and formidable, their icy dominance undeniable. Some were quite handsome, even edging on beautiful, but the evil within them

11

tarnished all of it. Kendrick…yes, he had that same dominance, and she knew he had crushed more than one foe, but something about him…

Was it too much to hope he might bid on her and win?

She refused to get her hopes up. Tonight, she'd end up in a stranger's bed, and it would be far more than her virginity ripped away. She wasn't sure she'd survive it.

"It's time," her father growled, showing a side to her he normally hid from others. His rough fingers dug into her arm as he "helped" her from the dais and guided her toward the stage. She gritted her teeth to keep from making a sound. She'd probably have bruises from his treatment. Somehow, she didn't think the men here would care.

Remember Jade, she told herself.

That was the only reason she was doing this. Her little sister. Moriah couldn't give a damn about her father. She certainly didn't love him. She'd seen woman after woman parading through his bed, even while her mother had been dying from ovarian cancer. But her sister. Moriah would do anything for her. Anything to keep her safe. And that included keeping her father out of prison until Moriah could get herself situated to get custody of Jade and raise her properly. God help her, that little girl would never be in the position Moriah had now had forced upon her.

"You could smile a little."

"Why?" she snapped. For once in her life, she wasn't being the good little girl and doing whatever he wanted. Where had that gotten her? Practically naked in front of a crowd of lascivious people, none of whom had her interests in mind. To them, her only worth was that tiny bit of flesh marking her pure.

Her cheeks burned hotter as she recalled the horrible examination she'd been subjected to, the doctors with their clinical demeanor and cold hands, even through the gloves they'd worn. She'd felt like livestock going to market. And wasn't she now?

"You know why. Stop acting like a martyr. You willingly agreed to this."

"Your memory is convenient, *Daddy*," she snapped.

"Don't get mouthy with me. No one here will give a shit if I turn you over my knee and redden that prudish ass of yours. Hell, half the men here would love it—would probably whip out their dicks and jerk off while I blistered your rear. Is that what you want?"

13

That was definitely something she didn't want. "Sorry," she murmured, if only to appease him lest he carry out the threat. Her father was more unpredictable than usual this evening.

"I should do it anyway," he grumbled. "It might actually increase the number of bids we get."

Her gaze slid momentarily to Kendrick. Would he care? Would he stop her father? Probably not. He just wanted his money and was probably there to ensure that it happened, that he was reimbursed for all that was embezzled from him.

Stop thinking about him! No one's here to save you. This isn't some twisted fairytale with a happily ever after. There is no prince on a white horse.

Her teeth clenched again, but she didn't smile. She swallowed and wished her mouth weren't so dry. Her father had handed her something to drink earlier, but she hadn't taken even a sip of it. He wanted her compliant and to get as much for her as he could. For that reason, she wouldn't put it past him to have put something in the amber-colored alcohol he'd given her.

All too soon, she stood in the center of the makeshift stage that had been constructed for this farce. Dread filled Moriah, and she closed her

14

eyes, clenching her fists before she forced herself to relax. She wondered what saint she should pray to for protection then immediately let that thought go. No saint would come to this lavish hell on earth. She was on her own.

Opening her eyes, she tried to appear dispassionate as she surveyed the supposedly cultured crowd before her. Seriously? A blond-haired man in the front row, not so subtly rubbed himself as he stared at her, only making a cursory effort to hide the action behind his auction paddle. Bidder Four. She wondered if that member he stroked was even four inches. What sort of man participated in this sort of thing?

A depraved man with no regard for humanity. That's who.

"Welcome everyone," Jof called, before he was handed a microphone. "Welcome," he repeated. "Everyone knows why we're here. I'm honored to grant one of you the opportunity to initiate my daughter into womanhood."

Honored? That was the direction he'd bend this? That they were doing him some favor?

"At a price, of course," he added, to which there were some chuckles. "Each of you bidding was tested as you entered. Moriah has also been inspected. The reports, along with a brief dossier

15

about her, are in the folder you were given when you entered. Now, the rules…"

Moriah's whole body clenched, the fine hairs on her arms lifting as her skin crawled. Yes, the rules. There were guidelines for this weekend, but she highly doubted any of those here would comply with anything they didn't want.

Unable to keep her head up, though she hadn't really done anything other than stare over the crowd since she'd seen the man fondling himself, she now focused on the wood surface below her. Her stomach roiled. Good thing she hadn't eaten. In fact, she hadn't eaten since she'd been blackmailed into this. Every time she considered it, she just heaved. The lack made her a little woozy now, but honestly, what did it matter.

"First, the winner forfeits his prize if he does not pass the health test. Other rules to be signed off on: I will know where Moriah is at all times. You are not to take her out of the country or even out of the city you've designated as your location for the weekend," her father intoned. "Moriah is on the birth control shot, but you must still use protection. You may not record the transaction in any way. You may not drug her. The winner is the only one allowed to touch her, unless she freely consents otherwise."

16

Freely consents? Laughable coming from him.

"She's yours from the end of the auction until Monday morning, at which time, she is to be returned safely to her home. What happens in between is your business."

Still staring at her feet in the strappy fuck-me heels that were killing her, Moriah parted her lips slightly and took shallow breaths. Her tear ducts burned, but she refused to cry.

"Moriah," Jof said. "Take off your dress."

Her eyes went wide as she looked at him. "No," she whispered.

The mic dropped to his side. "Take off the fucking dress, Moriah," he rasped through his teeth. "Remember what I said. I think you could use a good spanking."

"I hate you."

He shrugged. "All children hate their parents at one time or another. Now stop fucking around and do what I said."

It didn't matter. She wasn't a person to him. To any of them.

Steeling herself, she reached for the skirt of her dress, raising it. Though it fit her close, there were no zippers or other fasteners, she just had to lift up and wiggle out. The fabric tickled the skin of her thighs as she fisted it, pulling it upward. She didn't go slow. This wasn't a striptease. She wanted it over with, quick and done like removing a bandage.

The cloth protested as she wrenched it up and away from her, hurling it to the floor. In only her tiny white panties, she glared at the man who'd fathered her. She despised him.

Jade, she reminded herself. *You're doing this to take care of Jade*. The money Moriah earned on her back this weekend ensured he'd stay out of prison, and in return, he agreed to sign over full custody of her little sister. He wouldn't send Jade to her drugged-up mother who'd given away her rights shortly after Jade was born, and he'd relinquish his.

He reached toward her breast as if to display it better for the crowd. "Touch me and the deal's off," Moriah threatened.

"But Jade," he reminded.

"I'll find another way to get her." If she really believed that, though, she wouldn't be here. "And you'll be in prison."

He shrugged as if he hadn't a care. "Let's start the bidding. Moriah, give a whirl so they all see the whole package."

She didn't whirl, but she turned quickly, again determined not to arouse the people there any more than they already were by a naked woman in this precarious situation.

"Do I have an opening bid?"

"One thousand."

What the hell?

Jof tilted his head and raised a brow, mirroring her thought. "Really, Tyler? I'm going to pretend I didn't hear that. Does someone have an opening bid—a better opening bid?"

Chapter Three

Kendrick was done. He was putting a stop to this now. "One hundred million." No one would get the satisfaction of placing a bid on Moriah if he could help it.

There were murmurs of awe. Billionaires or not, he doubted any there had ever paid that much money for a weekend piece of ass. A hundred million was spouse level money.

There was silence. Obvious silence. The auction was over before it had really begun. Jof didn't even bother asking for another bid—he knew as well as Kendrick did that there would be none. Maybe if he were selling her hand in marriage there would be more interest, but virginity alone did not usually command such a high price.

Still, Jof searched around as if to see if anyone would offer more without his prompting, and finding only stony stares, gave a curt nod to the official auctioneer who proceeded to tap his gavel lightly. He cleared his throat. "We have a winning bid for the grand sum of one-hundred million dollars."

Disgusted by the whole ordeal and ready to leave immediately, Kendrick pulled out his smartphone and arranged to have half the money moved over to the designated account—an account he'd researched. Thankfully, it belonged to Moriah and *not* Jof, since Kendrick wouldn't put it past the bastard to take the cash and run. The other half was due by the end of the weekend.

Despite the anticlimactic turn of events, the party slowly resumed, the celebration more muted than it was before the auction. Clients whispered and looked Kendrick's way.

Pocketing his phone, Kendrick watch as Moriah was helped off the stage by her father. When she tried to collect her gown, the bastard tugged her forward, forcing her to remain unclothed. When she tried to cover her breasts with her arm, Jof smacked her elbow down and muttered at her. She lowered her gaze as he led her around the room like a prized mare, putting her on display for the licentious bidders who didn't win as he thanked them for their attendance.

Kendrick waited impatiently then finally decided to go retrieve his prize. The poor girl was shaking.

"That was…impressive," Jof remarked on his approach. "Unbelievably, you now owe me money."

"No," Kendrick replied, taking Moriah's upper arm and pulling her away from her father. "I owe your daughter money. What she chooses to do with it is up to her." He removed his jacket and draped it over her shoulders before taking her hand and leading her away.

"Where are you taking her?" Jofre called out.

"Home." His home.

Kendrick told himself to slow down, as Moriah was practically running to keep up with his purposeful strides, but he was too angry to walk at a leisurely pace. He stormed out the front into the large circular drive and marched to the first manned car he saw. He put Moriah in the backseat of the black BMW despite the shocked protests of the driver. Kendrick removed his wallet and handed a wad of bills to the driver then he followed her in.

"We just need a ride to the jet port," he explained. "Nothing more."

"Yes, sir." The man pocketed the substantial tip and started the car. The landing strip where the private jets waited was only a few minutes away from the residence. The driver would make it back to the party before his employer noticed his absence.

Moriah said nothing. She simply held his jacket close like a lifeline and stared out the window into the darkness. He studied her, searching for words of comfort, but he had none. What could he say to excuse the events of the evening?

With a frustrated huff, he removed his phone to alert the pilot to ready his jet. They would be arriving momentarily.

"Thank you," she offered quietly. "I'm glad it's you. I don't know why it's you, but I'm glad it is."

"I don't know what you mean," he replied.

"To be my first lover."

"I will not be your first lover."

She nearly broke her neck she turned her head so fast. "You can't pawn me off on another without my consent."

He tried not to take umbrage. It was a reasonable concern given that her father sold her off. Yet, it still jarred that she thought so little of him.

"That's not my intention. You're released from the sex portion of the contract as far as I'm concerned. However, you will stay the designated three days at my home lest your father compel you into another auction purely out of greed."

"Then why did you buy me if you had no intention of sleeping with me?"

Was he imagining the hurt in her tone?

"I never expected you to pay me for your father's sins. And I sure as hell never expected you to be a martyr." Every time Kendrick thought about it, he wanted to shake some sense into her.

"You agreed—"

"I simply informed Jof he had three days to return the money, an offer I extended simply for your benefit. You were incredibly…distressed…by the possibility of your father doing hard time for embezzlement."

She lowered her eyes, and he knew there was more to it.

"Is there something you wish to share?"

"No," she said all too quickly. She turned back to the window. "I just hate him, is all," she whispered.

"Considering how you were crying at my feet the other day, I think otherwise. But if you sincerely feel this way, let me send the bastard to prison."

"No, no…"

Kendrick rubbed his hands through his hair, frustrated by the needless circling. What was he missing? "Moriah, you're wealthy in your own right now. You no longer need him."

"I'm paying the firm back—and you'll take my virginity. You paid for it, it is yours, and I demand you honor the contract. You *will* fuck me."

What was this misguided bullshit?! How asinine, immature… What an ungrateful and imprudent little… Did Miss Catholic Good Girl actually use the work fuck? He'd never even heard her use a swear word before.

26

The car slowed, and Kendrick exited before it even came to a complete stop. He had to. If not, he was going throttle her. He was going to bend her over his lap and bring down the wrath of God upon her perfect little derriere. This wasn't a game. A lesser man would give into her demand if only to teach her lesson.

Damn it. Remembering he was a gentleman first, he reined in his temper and offered his hand to help her from the vehicle. He figured the stress of the auction had obviously taken a toll on her. She was being stubbornly irrational at the moment, and from what he knew of her, that wasn't her nature. He needed to give her a pass.

He led her up the stairs to the jet, greeted the cabin staff, and once inside, guided her to a seat.

"I can tell you're upset," she said quietly.

"You have no idea," he muttered.

"I'm sorry."

For some reason, her apology pissed him off more.

"I just… You paid so much money for me," she said.

He left her then to check in with the flight crew and get his injured hand cleaned up. And to find the frustrating woman some clothes.

Chapter Four

Moriah couldn't believe she'd said that. She'd demanded Kendrick, the man she'd crushed on for so long, fuck her...and take her virginity. She face-planted in her hand as she watched him disappear past a partition.

Maybe it was the stress of the day — the past three days actually! Maybe it was that sometime between arriving on this small island and when Kendrick had "won" her, she'd decided to take control of her own destiny. Or maybe she was having a mental breakdown. Could be any of the above.

And now he'd deserted her on this luxury aircraft. Had she scared him away? Right. No. If she'd learned anything over the years, it was that nothing frightened Kendrick Bergana, and he deemed everything a challenge. It worked for him. He had billions upon billions from it. What he'd dropped to purchase her tonight was nothing to him. Certainly nothing for her to feel guilty over. So why was she so determined to follow through on what he'd bought?

Because she wanted him. That's why. It really had nothing to do with the auction and everything to do with what she wanted from the powerful, oh-so-beautiful man.

And he left me, she reminded herself. Not that he could go far. The private plane was large in comparison to some, with partitioned off sections much like what she'd seen in a documentary about Air Force One. Though the plane that had brought her here had been opulent, it had been half the size of Kendrick's.

He hadn't come back when a cabin attendant approached.

"We're about to take off. You'll need to fasten your seatbelt," the curvy woman said with a forced smile. Her cold eyes scanned over Moriah, making her feel uncomfortable. "Can I get you anything? A drink? A blanket?"

"A blanket, maybe," Moriah replied. What was with this woman? Her judgment and hostility were barely veiled.

"Scotch, Amy," Kendrick said as he returned. He dropped into the plush seat beside Moriah and handed her a jumble of fabric.

"Right away, Mr. Bergana," Amy gushed, her whole demeanor changing.

How clichéd could you get? Of course, his stewardess wanted him.

Moriah rolled her eyes and focused on the bundle Kendrick had dropped in her lap. It was a thick blanket, a pair of pajama pants and a T-shirt. She glanced over at him in question.

"I keep clothes onboard for overseas travel. Sometimes, I sleep, and I don't like to nap in my suit. If you want to rest, there's a bed in back."

She shook her head. Even if she were tired, she wanted to be near him.

"You can change once we're in the air," he told her. "Meanwhile, you can cover up with the blanket."

"I'm not cold," she said, being purposely difficult while she stretched out her bare legs. They weren't that long, given how short she was, but they were proportionately nice and rather shapely, if she did say so herself. She rather thought they were one of her best features. She pointed her shell-pink painted toes. She'd wanted red, but her father had insisted on something more "virginal" for her toes and fingers.

"For God's sake, Moriah," Kendrick muttered.

"What?" she asked, all the innocence.

"Will you please cover up?"

"You don't like what you see?"

"Moriah…"

"If you didn't want me, why did you buy me?"

"Would you keep your voice down? I don't need all my staff knowing about that—and if you don't think they'll talk, that the gossip will spread to who knows where, then you're dead wrong."

"Wouldn't want to besmirch your reputation."

"I'm thinking of yours, little brat. Now cover up before I put you over my knee and give them something to talk about."

She blinked at him, her mouth dropping open. "Did you just threaten to spank me?"

"I prefer to keep it in the bedroom, but yes. And I damn well will if you don't listen."

Moriah squirmed a little, strangely turned on by his threat and hoping her wet, barely covered sex didn't leave a mark on the jet's soft, leather seat. "Are you like one of those...domestic discipline men?"

He chuffed out a harsh laugh. "No. But I do like to do a little spanking and for my woman to obey me in the bedroom—and when it comes to things like protecting her, whether it's bodily or something like her modesty or reputation."

His woman?

That was an improvement over his intention not to touch her.

"Your woman?" she questioned aloud.

"You are for the weekend, aren't you? That's what a cool one-hundred mil says."

"But in the car—"

"In the car I said I didn't plan to take your virginity. You're still mine for the weekend."

"But what if I want you to?"

"Why?" he asked. "Because of that damn auction? Because of some misguided sense of responsibility?"

Though it took all her courage, more courage than to take off her dress in that roomful of men, Moriah told him the truth. "No, neither of those. I was telling the truth when I said I was glad it was you. I... Well, I want you. I have for a long time."

Kendrick studied her, his impassive face making her nervous, uncomfortable like a bug under a microscope. It didn't dull her need to be his. Even if it would be over by Monday morning, she'd still know what it was like to be with him, still know that her virginity belonged to him, that her first love had a part of her that she'd never get back, that she'd never want back.

"Okay," he finally said.

"Okay?" she echoed in disbelief. That was all he had to say.

"Yes. If that's what you really want, you'll be in my bed all weekend. But understand this: I'm giving you what you want on this issue, but it will be completely on my terms."

"All right," she agreed, feeling even wetter. Prickly heat swept through her, arousing her nerve endings as every bit of her reacted to him and homed in on everything that attracted her to Kendrick — which truthfully was *everything* about him.

"And you will obey me," he added.

She blinked at him, swallowing hard and feeling as if she'd just received a lot more than she'd bargained for. She looked down at the floor, her tongue swiping quickly over her bottom lip. The hand beneath the bundle of blanket, curled and uncurled into a fist on her thigh as tension climbed within her. If she said yes…

"Are you into…BDSM?" she asked.

"What do you know of it?"

"I read," she replied, conveying with her tone that she wasn't stupid.

"Then you know what a dominant is? And a submissive?"

Had she thought her mouth was dry before? "Y-y-yes."

"I'm not into whips and chains and all the paraphernalia," he said to her relief. It was short-lived. "But I do like a little spanking, as I said. And bondage. And complete obedience and control in bedroom matters. *Your* obedience. *My* control."

"Okay." She wasn't sure what else to say.

"You understand?"

"Yes."

"And you will obey me?" he repeated.

Would she? Could she take this step? Was this…negotiation?

"Do I have to call you something special? Master? Sir? Mr. Bergana?"

"No. Just Kendrick if you feel like it—never Ken." Somehow, she'd gotten the feeling that grated on him. He was so far from a *Ken*.

"Okay…Kendrick," she replied, trying it on for size and liking it. She'd always called him that in her fantasies. Of course, she had. And she'd been Moriah Bergana—but that was another story and one that wouldn't come to fruition. She'd just take what she could and revel in the experience.

"And you will obey me?" he repeated, and this time she got the feeling if he had to ask again, she would be over his knee for God and the world to see.

"Yes," she agreed. "Yes, I'll obey you."

"Good." A small smile lifted one side of his lips. "Now, first things first. As soon as we're in the air, you'll go change. Then you'll behave until we get home to my place. Lesson one, my little virgin, I don't share. Not the sight of things meant only for me, not your touch, not even the sound of your pleasure—or discipline. What I desire, what you desire, is private and remains in *private*."

Right. He didn't want anyone to know what he did away from the public eye. What he'd done tonight had already been overt enough.

She nodded, agreeing. This might be far more than she'd ever imagined, but suddenly, it was everything she'd ever wanted. Tonight, she'd finally be in Kendrick's bed and belonging to him. It wouldn't be just sex. It would be ownership.

Chapter Five

Unable to concentrate, Kendrick threw his phone on a table and wondered for a thousandth time how he could so easily be goaded into sex by a virgin. Where was his backbone? Where was his self-control?

He rubbed the tension from his brow. Honestly, he should be ashamed by how quickly he'd caved into her ridiculous demand that he see the contract through. Instead of diffusing the situation, he let himself be swayed by her confession.

"I want you. I have for a long time."

He replayed those words again and again in his head, and his cock ached from imagining the possibilities of the weekend to come.

"And you will obey me?"

"Yes, I'll obey you."

He looked to where Moriah lay curled in her seat, snuggled deep into a blanket and snoring ever-so quietly like a purring kitten. She'd never even changed out of his jacket. The clothes he'd given her when they'd arrived had become a pillow not long after takeoff, and she was asleep before the jet had finished its ascent. She'd slept the whole flight. He could only imagine the stress that asshole Jofre had put her through the past few days. She was probably mentally and physically exhausted. He couldn't help smiling though. She knew she was safe with him. If not, she would have fought sleeping.

In a few minutes, they'd begin descent. They would land, and soon she'd be in his car. Then in his home. Then in his bed…

"I want you. I have for a long time."

When Moriah was younger, Kendrick hadn't pay her much mind. He'd been too busy to be concerned with childish things. But since Moriah had graduated from high school, he'd seen more of her around the office—and his libido had taken notice of the woman she'd become. She was so unlike the other females he encountered from day-to-day. She was authentic from her shoes to her personality. What you saw was what you got, and it was enticingly low maintenance, especially for someone of her affluent upbringing.

Possessing her was something he'd secretly fantasized about from time-to-time, especially in the last few months, but he'd denied himself ever pursuing her in reality. Besides, she was Jofre's daughter, she was innocent and far too inexperienced for the more dominant passions he enjoyed.

Or so he'd thought.

"You'll take my virginity. You paid for it, it is yours, and I demand you honor the contract. You will fuck me."

Kendrick remembered Jof once complaining about his prudish daughter, something that had bothered Kendrick at the time, but he eventually chalked up to Jof's mercenary ways. When it came to money, nothing was off the table for Jof, including using his daughter to get ahead with clients. "She's still a damn virgin," Jof had lamented. "She's never been kissed much less fucked by a man. I should have removed her from St. Agnes the moment her mother died. Who the hell waits for marriage anymore?"

What kind of man said that about his daughter? If it had been up to Kendrick, Jof would have been gone from the firm a long time ago. But the Board of Directors liked him. It wasn't a personality contest, they had reasoned. Profit is the goal, they had preached.

Amy, the flight attendant in charge, sashayed her way over to him. "Mr Bergana, we'll be landing momentarily. Is there anything I can get you?" she asked cheerily.

"No, thank you," he murmured, placing a finger over his lips and tilting his head toward Moriah.

Amy smiled brightly in understanding and acknowledgment of his sleeping companion. "Very well," she whispered with a nod. However, when she turned to return to the galley, he caught the shade she threw Moriah.

Ah. This would be a problem.

Kendrick retrieved his phone and sent the assistant in charge of his traveling logistics a text. Besides requesting a secure limousine to be waiting rather than his usual car since he'd need the privacy, he also arranged to have his penthouse stocked with food and ordered that the staff vacated it by his arrival.

Also, request a new flight crew for all future flights.

True, he was unhappy with only one member of the team, but a team they were, and as a team, the crew would be reassigned to another contract. Moriah might only be his for the weekend, but he protected what was his, and that included protecting what was his from little green monsters. Not that Kendrick worried Amy would harm Moriah, but why bother with the discomfort. While this wasn't the first time Kendrick had been on the receiving side of a crush, he demanded self-discipline and professionalism from all contractors and employees, and Amy was lacking both.

The jet landed smoothly, allowing Moriah to sleep through that, as well. He almost hated waking her since he was sure she'd hadn't slept much the last few days.

"Come, kitten," he said as he helped her to her feet. He kept the blanket wrapped around her as she groggily followed his lead out the plane. As requested, a limo waited. The well-dressed chauffeur, who also doubled as his security, had the door already open.

He guided Moriah into the back the luxury vehicle and took position across from her. With the privacy partition up and locked between the chauffeur and the passenger compartment, Kendrick used the intercom to communicate his desires to the driver then muted the system.

Moriah seemed content to just look out the window. It was only after they were on the road for while that she finally spoke.

"Where are we going?" she asked.

She sounded hoarse, so Kendrick gave her a bottle of water. She took it with a small smile and thanked him for his consideration.

"We're going to my home," he answered.

"Which one?"

He lifted a brow. "I only have one home. The other houses you've visited with your father are simply places where I host events, conduct business, etcetera."

"Oh," she nodded.

Kendrick took a moment to study her. She was beautiful, even when sleepy. But something wasn't quite right...

He collected a linen square from the small drink cabinet and moistened it with bottled water. He crossed over to her side of the limo. Surprised and wide eyed, she leaned away as he lifted the napkin toward her face.

"No, no, no," he said. "You are mine for the weekend. Stay put."

Moriah bit her lower lip as she returned upright, and the urge to kiss her was near unbearable. But he held back. There was no rush. And he didn't want to scare her. He simply wanted to remove some of the makeup she was wore, a reminder of the auction and how her father had exploited her, trying to force her to be something she was not—a whore.

Gently, he wiped away the heavy eye makeup, some of which had smudged beneath while she'd slept. With a clean portion of the fabric, he swiped away the blood-red lipstick to reveal as much of her natural lip color as possible, though they were stained from the tint. It was still better than it had been.

She seemed surprised again when he folded the napkin and returned to his seat across from her. He tried to smile. "Did you expect me to ravish you?"

Rolling her eyes, she grinned. "Yes. I guess I did. I don't know."

"I'm going to ask you a very personal question, and I want—no, *need*—you to be completely honest with me."

"Okay," she answered. "I can do that."

"What's your level of experience with men?" he asked.

"None. Hence the auction."

"Have you ever held hands with a man?"

"In an intimate fashion? No."

"Have you kissed a man?"

"No."

"May I ask why?"

She released a heavy exhale. "I went to a very strict, all-girls catholic boarding school in the middle of nowhere. When I graduated and returned home, I...had no inclination to date, no matter how much my father insisted I should earn my keep by entertaining some of his clients."

Hearing that pissed him off. What the hell was wrong with Jofre? Besides the embezzling, apparently a lot of things.

"I..." She lowered her gaze. "I wanted something...or someone...more."

The *"someone"* wasn't lost on him. "Why? Until the last few months, we didn't interact very much."

Moriah shrugged. "You were always nice to me. You always treated me with respect. You didn't require anything of me. You were kind to my mother, which my father was not."

He wrinkled his nose in distaste. "So I can chalk this up to daddy issues?"

She burst into laughter. "God, no. You're also pretty hot. And not even close to old enough to be my father."

He chuckled. "Well, you won me for the weekend. So let us begin."

"You won me."

Kendrick shook his head. "No, you convinced me to honor the contract you could have walked away from without penalty."

"You make me feel like I'm in the position of power."

"You are," he agreed. "You will be all weekend. You also agreed to obey me in all things. That's where your power lies."

"How so?"

"Remove the blanket and jacket, please. Right now. Hand both to me."

Her eyes widened as her ease faltered. She looked out the windows and back at him then back again to the outside, as if to compel him into seeing all the traffic and people walking around downtown. He didn't have to look. He knew they were there.

"Moriah. Blanket and jacket," he reiterated. "Please give them to me."

She didn't move to follow his directions. She simply lowered her gaze. He sucked his teeth in disappointment and shook his head. "Naughty girl. Do you remember what I said to you in the plane right after you said, 'Yes, I'll obey you.'?"

"What?" she whispered.

"I don't share. Not the sight of things meant only for me, not your touch, not even the sound of your pleasure — or discipline. What I desire, what you desire, is private and remains in *private*," he repeated verbatim. "You failed your first test."

He immediately saw he'd hurt her feelings. She looked simultaneously frustrated and crestfallen at the same time.

"There are people everywhere!"

"Kitten, we're in the back of a locked limo with the darkest tint allowed. We can see out. No one can see in." He exhaled heavily. "For our weekend to be pleasurable — for both of us — you

48

need to trust me. If you can't trust me, then we shouldn't be intimate."

With a huff, Moriah tore off the blanket and tossed it to him. The jacket followed a moment later. Kendrick wanted to take her to task for the outburst, but she sat there in nothing but heels, diamonds, and underwear, and fuck, she was gorgeous.

"I do trust you," she declared. "You saved me. You're the only person I trust in this world."

Her admission moved him more than it should have. "How do you feel?" he asked.

"Vulnerable."

"Good. Anything else?"

"Like?"

"Excitement?"

Though he saw her embarrassment, she didn't look away. "Yes. Even though no one can see inside, there's still an element of danger." She then stared him down. "How do you feel?"

Oh, he liked this. He liked her brat side very much. "Aroused."

"Anything else?" she retorted.

"I feel like I want to slip off your pretty white panties and feast on your pussy."

He said it to shock her, to teach her lesson about attitude, and he received the response he wanted. She turned beet red.

Her chest heaved. "Do it."

Kendrick grinned. "There's an order to things like this. You've never even experienced a passionate kiss before—"

"Yes, I have."

It was his turn to be shocked. "You told me—"

"You asked if I'd ever kissed a man. And I said no. I have been kissed, though, by a girl."

"Intriguing," he said quietly. "Did this woman do anything else besides kiss you?"

Moriah shrugged it off. "She was a friend at the academy. She kissed me. And put her hand up my shirt. Nothing more. I...I just wasn't into girls like she was. It was fine with me that she was into girls. I just...wasn't."

He nodded in understanding. "What did you think of the experience?"

"It was nice, just..." Moriah looked out the window. "Like I told you earlier, I wanted someone else more."

Kendrick left his seat and knelt before her. "Are you sure? We've not even had our first kiss yet."

She nodded. "Yes, please."

Chapter Six

Kendrick didn't reach for her panties as she'd expected. Instead, he wedged himself between her thighs, which she spread wide to accommodate him then he lifted a hand to cup the back of her head, drawing her forward.

"I believe in having an order to things," he murmured against her lips, and she shivered at the featherlight touch against her skin. "Before you learn what it's like to have a man take your pussy, what my mouth will feel like when I devour you, you need to learn what it's like when a man kisses you."

"Oh God," Moriah gasped, wanting to press her legs together to relieve the throbbing that erupted with his nearness, his words an accelerant that could burst her into flames. She squirmed on the seat, but Kendrick's other hand gripped her hip and kept her still.

"You're mine, kitten. Tell me to stop, that you've changed your mind, because from this moment on, there's no escaping me."

"Don't stop," she begged.

He moved even closer, and she moaned at the feel of his starched suit jacket rubbing against her hard nipples. Kendrick took advantage, diving in and claiming her mouth. He didn't wait to be invited in. His tongue delved inside, sliding against hers, possessing her mouth as his lips moved hungrily against hers. Pulling back, he nipped at her bottom lip the he dove back in, his hand at her nape angling her for his pleasure.

Moriah thrust both hands into his lush hair, stretching up to get closer to him. The movement pushed her breasts against his chest again, and the fabric once more abrading the tips. A heavy, unfamiliar ache filled her sex, and she knew a need she'd never once experienced before, not even in her darkest fantasies about this man. And all this from a kiss.

He was right. It was so different from the clumsy, nubile groping she'd engaged in that one time with her friend. Kendrick knew what he wanted, and he was taking it all. There was no denying his rough dominance even as he was gentle with her. But she wanted it, all of it, everything he'd give her.

They were panting hard, and her lips felt swollen when he pulled back. He stared into her eyes. Never breaking his gaze, he pressed his mouth to her upper breast then down the inner slope, up to the peak.

"Oh, God, yes," she cried as he drew hard on the ruched tip. She pushed into him, her hands holding his head there. Each pull of his mouth seemed to yank a line directly connected to her core, and she knew she was getting slick with her need for him. He'd find her so wet when he drew off her panties and pressed this wicked mouth there.

Letting go with a pop, he repeated the action with the other nipple.

"Just a taste of what's to come," he said. Then, still keeping eye contact, he continued kissing down her middle to her belly. The intimacy of it bound them together. It was just them. No one and nothing else existed. She knew he wanted to watch her reactions, that despite what he'd said, he was checking her willingness every step of the way. Oh, yes, she was willing. So willing. So ready for him to just fuck her.

His tongue circled her navel, and she shivered, goose bumps lifting along her skin as he aroused her. Then he was at her waistband.

"Last chance, kitten," he said.

Moriah shook her head. "All my chances were gone a long time ago."

He smirked, pulling back and forcing her hands from his hair as he moved from between her legs. Her arms dropped to her sides as his fingers went to the thin elastic keeping the silk in place.

"I think mine were gone, too," he admitted, and that admission warmed her in a far different way than the heavy sexual tension surrounding them. He made her feel special. Wanted. That she was his, but he was hers, too.

She halfway expected him to rip away the panties, but he didn't. Of course he didn't. Kendrick was far too methodical and controlled than that. While the ripping might have been exciting, nothing compared to the anticipation that built inside her as he slowly dragged the minuscule fabric down her legs. Her breaths were shaky as she watched the progression, watched his face as he stripped away that last bit from her body, leaving her in just the diamonds and her shoes. The heels were pulled off and tossed aside a moment later.

"Eventually, I'll fuck you in them," he commented as the second Manolo dropped from his hand, "but as this is your first time with my mouth on you, I don't want to take the chance you'll stab me with one."

"I wouldn't!"

"No on purpose."

"What do you — oh my God!" she exclaimed as he shoved her legs apart and pushed his mouth into her folds. His hands immediately parted her for better access as his tongue circled her clit.

"I like that you're waxed," he said against her, never letting up on eating.

"I… He thought… Oh, Kendrick," she gasped. Her fingers clenched into the seat, her head thrown back as he kissed her pussy as fervently as he had her mouth. She'd touched herself in the past but nothing — *nothing* — compared to the actuality of him…devouring her.

"Jesus, you taste like heaven. And to think I almost let you go." He took a long lap at her center, his fingers playing at her opening. Then he caught her clit in his lips again and one digit, slowly worked inside her. It was barely the tip but her body exploded, colors flashing across her vision as she convulsed against that foreign bit of his body invading her. The pleasure shocked her, and she cried out, arching, her legs drawing up to push him away. Kendrick shoved them open and back, resting her feet on the edge of the bench and holding her there as he continued his feast.

She moaned, her head rolling back and forth on the seat back. "Feels...to good," she moaned. "I can't..."

"You can," he growled. "You will." Then he bit down lightly on that sensitive bundle of nerves he'd been tormenting. His finger pushed deeper, then pulled back, mimicking what he'd do later. If this overwhelmed her, she couldn't imagine what would happen later. "You're so fucking tight. Your tight little pussy will strangle me when I get in there."

"Hug you," she gasped, trying to joke when most of her brain cells were centered under his mouth. He chuckled, the vibration drawing a groan from her.

"One hell of a hug."

"Wanted you for so long."

"Then be a good girl and come for me again. I want to taste more of that sweet cream all over my tongue."

"I—" A scream erupted, stopping her denial. He'd twisted the finger and found a spot inside her that sent stars sparkling across her vision and just like that she shook, arching as ecstasy swamped her.

When she came back to herself, Kendrick had her on his lap, his arms around her. He rocked her, crooning to her as he petted her hair. "Such a perfect little kitten," he whispered.

She buried her face in his neck, breathing in his spicy masculine scent. Clean and woodsy and all Kendrick.

"I never imagined," she whispered.

"That's just the start."

"Hmm," she sighed. "I'm glad it was you."

* * * *

Moriah realized she must have fallen asleep, or at least into a deep daze, because the next she knew, Kendrick was carrying her and she was wrapped in the blanket like a giant burrito.

"Where are we?" she murmured, taking in the marble and subdued lighting—or at least as much as she could without lifting her head from Kendrick's chest.

"My building. My penthouse is on the top floor. This is my private entry."

While she watched, he pressed his palm to panel beside the gold-toned elevator doors, and a moment later, the doors whispered open. As soon as he'd carried her inside, they closed just as quietly.

"Penthouse," he said, then the lift whooshed upward. He kissed her temple. "Voice control. Very handy when carrying such a precious bundle."

She smiled into his lapel. "I hope it understands better than Siri."

He laughed. But then the door opened and he was carrying her inside his home. Keeping her as off-balance as ever, he didn't take her to his bedroom as she'd expected. Instead, he took her to the kitchen and deposited her in one of the tall chairs beside the bar.

"It's been a long day," he said. "First some water; then some rest."

"But—"

He caught her chin and brought it up to him. "Some rest," he reiterated. "But if you think I'm not going to fuck you, my little virgin, you're very wrong. I prefer wide awake to a zombie, though. You've had a rough few days. Tonight you'll sleep in my arms, and tomorrow... Well, we'll let tomorrow bring what it will."

Turning away, he went to the refrigerator and grabbed two bottles of water. He handed her one, then twisted off the cap on his own. She stared at him, watching his throat as he swallowed. She bit her lip, doing her own swallowing as she imagined her mouth on him there.

His chin lowered and he stared at her, lifting a brow. "Drink."

She made a face. "Yes, sir."

"Perhaps you're not too tired for a spanking, brat."

Moriah quickly opened her bottle and brought it to her lips. Much as it intrigued her, she wasn't so sure she wanted to test him. "I'll be good," she said after a couple sips.

"I know you will."

And his smirk made her believe they weren't speaking about the same thing, Then heat

61

flooded her face. After what they'd done, she shouldn't be embarrassed when he talked about sex. Still…

She drank a bit more to hide her discomfort.

He crushed his bottle and put it in recycling. "We'll have to get you some clothes."

"We do? I mean, we will?"

Kendrick nodded, his arms crossed over his chest as he watched her. "As enticing as it is, I don't want you running around here naked the next few days." He leaned closer. "Believe it or not, I have more in mind than sex with you."

"You probably have to work." She imagined, as successful as he was, that he worked continually.

"No. But I probably want to take you out." He shrugged. "Have some fun."

She blinked at him. "Really? Like…like a…date?"

He looked at the ceiling and tilted his head back and forth as if weighing the word. "More or less. Yeah."

"I'd like that."

"Good. Done?" he asked, nodding his head toward her empty bottle. She handed it to him and he disposed of it as he had his own. Coming around the island, he held out his hand. "And now, rest."

He took her hand and she stood, leaving the blanket behind. "Leave it," he said when she went to grab it. "No one's here. You don't need to wrap up."

Well, no one but him, but she guessed he *had* had his face between her legs less than a half hour ago.

She followed behind him as he led her through the spacious penthouse. Though large and well-appointed, it wasn't a showplace. He obviously lived here, and she wouldn't be afraid of tripping a breaking something priceless. The space was open, with high ceilings and huge windows overlooking the city. The dark leather furnishings were obviously high-quality, but again, they looked comfortable and meant to be used. She could easily see curling up on one of the big couches and reading a book with the sun streaming in on her.

He led her down a wide hallway, laid with thick cream-colored carpet. Various works of art hung along the long expanse of walls, with narrow tables beneath, topped with sprays of greenery.

"Are these all bedrooms?" she asked after they'd passed the fifth doorway.

"No, the first was my office." They turned a corner and came immediately to a set of double doors. "Our bedroom," he said opening one and ushering her inside.

Our bedroom? Well, at least for the weekend, right?

Like the rest of the house, the room was spacious. Nothing about his penthouse seemed closed in. His quarters were easily three times the size of her own back home, with an enormous king-sized bed she'd need a boost into and a sitting area by the windows.

As she looked around wide-eyed, she felt very much like the country mouse in city mouse digs. She'd grown up with wealth but Kendrick's living space, though probably smaller than her father's mansion in overall square footage, made her childhood home look...poor in comparison. Billions compared to a few million, she guessed. All the rooms here were sprawling, and everything seemed so new and plush and perfectly appointed. Yet nothing seemed "trying too hard." She was also familiar with that since everything her father did was meant to impress.

"Let's get you something to wear," Kendrick said and brought her into the closet that was at least the size of her bedroom at home. He opened a cedar drawer and pulled out a T-shirt. He didn't hand it to her, but instead, slid it on her. It hung almost to her knees, covering all of her. She watched as he slipped out of his coat and draped it over the bench in the center of the room.

"You can go climb in bed," he said as he pulled on his tie.

She crossed her arms and tilted her head. "I'd rather stay here."

"Really?" he laughed, tossing the tie over his suit coat then reaching for the buttons of his shirt.

"I've been parading around naked. I think it's fair to see what I'm getting."

He grinned, shaking his head and continuing to unbutton. She sighed when he pulled off his shirt to reveal a T-shirt beneath.

"How many layers are you wearing?" she griped.

He raised an eyebrow and unfastened his belt, and she found she rather liked this striptease of his. Her fingers curled into her shirt as she imagined crossing the space and helping him. She caught her breath as he unzipped then toed off his shoes and socks. The pants dropped, and he stepped free, leaving him in black boxer-briefs and the white undershirt. Her mouth watered as she took in his muscular legs and trailed her gaze up to the bulge pushing against the front of his underwear. As she stared, she almost missed him yanking off the shirt to reveal sculpted perfection, complete with a six-pack he had to work hard for.

And they weren't having sex tonight? She wanted to learn every bit of him, to touch him and feel all that warm, golden skin beneath her palms. She wanted those slim hips between her legs again, like they had been in the car, but this time without clothes.

She'd waited so long for him. So long... She should be startled by her less than innocent thoughts, but she wasn't. Too many nights she'd pictured him with her. Never had her fantasies matched this.

His grin widened at her ogling, and he came toward her. "Come on, kitten," he murmured. "Time for bed before we both get in trouble."

She stumbled after him. "But maybe I want trouble."

He stopped abruptly and she ran into him. She groaned as her cheek flattened against his warm skin. He turned and she was face-to-face with muscled pec. If she just leaned forward a smidgen, she could—

He caught her chin, bringing her gaze to his. "Uh-uh. It's been a long, emotional day." He scooped her up into his arms then deposited her onto the bed. She scooted beneath the blankets as he circled to the other side. When he climbed in, he pulled her back against his chest, spooning her, his erection pressing against her behind, his arms tight around her. She savored the sensations, his heat, the feel of him surrounding her, his soft breath against her hair, the steady rise and fall of his chest, safety…

Maybe, he was right. She was tired.

"Goodnight, my sweet Moriah," he murmured, but she couldn't answer. She was too far gone, on her way to dreams filled with him.

Chapter Seven

Kendrick rose from the bed before the sun touched the horizon. It was his way. He enjoyed the peace of the early morning hours. He threw on some sweats and made his way to the kitchen to brew a pot of coffee. While it percolated, he leaned against the marble counter island and used his phone to check his email and answer messages. He also ordered clothes for Moriah to be delivered by 9:00AM.

He pondered what he'd do about Jofre. Kendrick might have allowed Jof to quietly retire with forfeiture of benefits had he been a decent human being and simply returned the money. After all, no organization wanted the intrusive inspection and media attention a scandal like embezzlement brought. Fraud charges made clients and shareholders nervous and was bad for business. Instead, Jof had decided selling his daughter to raise the funds was a clever idea. That made Kendrick simply want to turn the bastard in to the authorities and be done with it.

"Hey," he heard from behind him.

Kendrick turned to find Moriah, sleep-tousled in his T-shift, making her way to his coffeemaker.

"You're up early," he said. As she poured her coffee, he resisted the urge to press up behind her and kiss her neck, his hands roaming their way under the shirt—pulling it over her head. That way she'd be naked and ready for him, and he could bend her over and slide his hard cock deep into her warmth.

But not yet.

Her first time wouldn't be a morning quickie in his kitchen. He'd do it right, make her first time special for her, and do his level best to erase the previous night's events from her memory. He wanted her to have no regrets.

He watched her and noted she liked her coffee light and sweet, like her personality. He loved that about her. He knew for a fact she tasted sweet, too.

She joined him at the kitchen island, taking a seat on one of the stools. "I usually get up early, but even for me this is a bit before my normal wake up time. I must have missed you," she mused.

Aww. That touched him with unusual warmth. She was going to turn him into a sap.

"Are you hungry?" he asked.

"Starved," she admitted.

"I'll make you breakfast," he declared, moving toward the refrigerator. He opened the door and proceeded to remove ingredients for an omelet. He also took out some strawberries.

"Oh. Um…" Moriah smiled. "Thank you. It's very kind of you to want to cook for me, but I'm vegan, so fruit is just fine for me. Promise."

"Oh." Kendrick returned all the non-vegan items to the refrigerator. "I'm actually vegetarian, but I know a few vegan recipes. I'll make you something. Fruit isn't enough." Especially with what he had planned for her.

"Do you like to cook?"

He nodded. "I do. It's my guilty pleasure."

While he cooked, they chatted about other hobbies they both enjoyed and secret talents they both possessed. He was thrilled by how easily the conversation flowed and how light and fun it was. It had been a long time since he laughed so much.

During the meal, the conversation turned to quieter, more mundane things like studies and work. They avoided discussion of her father or the auction, for which he was grateful. It was almost too easy to forget that they weren't dating. To his surprise, being with Moriah just felt...right. Last night, he'd wanted to save her. Today, well, he was beginning to think he might want to keep her.

When they'd finished the last of breakfast, Kendrick retrieved the rosewater-infused berries from the fridge, which he topped with a dollop of whipped coconut cream.

He purposely brought one spoon with him to the kitchen island. "May I have the pleasure of feeding you?"

She smiled. "You're asking, but do I have a choice?" She opened her mouth to receive a spoonful.

"Unless you have a sincere and valid reason why I shouldn't, I expect you to say yes." He fed her again.

"What happens if I don't do what you want this weekend?"

"Again, if you have a sincere and valid reason, we'll talk. I'm not an ogre. But if you're just being a brat, what do you think?" he asked.

"I have a feeling the threat you made on the plane, that you'd spank me, is one you'd follow through."

Kendrick nodded. "You're correct."

"Why?"

He sent the question back to her. "It's who I am. But tell me, why shouldn't I?"

She shrugged. "Because it will hurt."

"So will it when I take your virginity."

Moriah frowned and made a disgruntled little sound. "That's different."

"It is? It all leads to feeling good. What if I promised to follow it with pleasure?" He brought the spoon back to her mouth. Moriah's tongue darted out to lick her lips before she accepted his offering. They ate in silence for a few minutes, and she seemed to be thinking.

"We should shower," she said suddenly. "Together."

Surprised, Kendrick dropped the spoon in the bowl, and it bounced with a clank. Apparently, she wasn't thinking what he'd thought. "What made you decide that?"

"I just think we should get acquainted with each other's bodies before we sleep together. Plus, I really just want a shower."

Picking up the spoon, he gave her the last bite of berries then got up and deposited the bowl in the sink. Things were moving faster with Moriah than he'd anticipated, and he really wanted more time to set up a special night for her, but why not indulge her desire? Some of the best things in life were unplanned, so the saying goes, and surely, he could control himself — and her — from going too far.

"All right. Follow me."

Kendrick led her to the large master bathroom. He retrieved extra toiletries from the drawer of the two-person vanity and gathered towels from the cabinet.

"Feel free to use whatever you need. Then come in here." He showed her to the bathing area. Moriah seemed in awe of the luxurious room. His favorite part was the rainfall shower area, but she seemed focused on the enormous soak tub.

Though the floor was heated, he turned on the fireplace for her.

"Would you prefer a bath?"

"No, no," she said wistfully. "Maybe another day. I want to shower…with you."

Nodding, he said, "I'll be back shortly. Enjoy until I return." He then left her to bathe.

Back in his office, Kendrick contacted the designer he'd chosen to dress Moriah and arranged to have her new clothes delivered immediately, much to the delight of the designer who seemed more than happy to drop off the collection himself since Kendrick promised to pay extra for the trouble. Then, he contacted his weekend personal assistant. He instructed her to make lunch reservations at his favorite restaurant. Also, she was also to arrange a chef to come in and prepare dinner for a seven PM mealtime— and he needed roses. He wanted lots of candles and roses throughout the kitchen, bedroom, and bathroom. And the bathtub filled.

"I need all this to happen by seven tonight. And don't let me down. I'm trying to impress a lady."

"No problem, Mr. Bergana. It will be perfect," his upbeat assistant promised. "She'll fall in love with you by the time I'm done."

Kendrick laughed. "Well, yes, I guess that would be nice. Thank you."

After he hung up, he returned to the bathroom to find Moriah already in the shower. Beyond the glass and steam, her naked body glistened under the water drops tumbling from the ceiling like a summer rain shower. She stared up at the spray, allowing the water to cascade down her form like a slow-motion movie scene.

His cock immediately hardened. This was a very bad idea. He turned to leave, but she spotted him.

"Get undressed," she called. "This shower is perfect."

Cursing his luck but unable to disappoint her, he disrobed and joined her. Upon seeing his cock standing proudly, her eyes widened. She stared. "Oh my God, it's so big." To his surprise, she reached out and drew her fingers along his length.

He nearly spewed at the featherlight touch. Damn her innocent charms.

"Okay. That's enough," he groused. Gently, he turned her around so her back and beautiful ass were to him.

"Did I do something wrong?" she asked.

The humor in her tone wasn't lost on him. Little brat. She might be a virgin, but she obviously wasn't a blushing one. At least not at the moment. Moriah seemed to know exactly what she wanted and how to get it. What exactly was in those books she'd read?

"No," he replied. He poured shampoo in his hands then lathered her hair.

"Then why did you stop me?" She sighed as she leaned her head into his touch.

"Stop you from what?" He knew what she meant, but he was going to make her say it aloud.

"Touching your... You know, touching it."

"It?" he laughed.

"You know what I mean."

Kendrick guided her to rinse her hair. "If you want something from me, just ask."

"I want to touch your penis," she blurted, her voice rising nearly an octave. She was obviously a little embarrassed stating her desires aloud, but she was braving her way through the experience. He'd reward her for that.

"You can wash me while you explore," he said and put the soap in her hand.

She turned to face him with a smile. He returned it and stood there in all his naked glory, his cock so fucking hard it was damn near pointing at her in accusation.

Moriah bit her lip and lathered the soap in her hands. Then, looking him in the eyes, she proceeded to clean his chest. Kendrick was never one to be unsettled by a stare down, but hell, her eyes — all sparkling and mischievous — were something beautiful to behold. It would be *waaay* too easy to fall for her. He needed to be careful. He only had her for the weekend.

But why couldn't it be longer? He'd thought about her far more than he should for the past few years, and it had taken him less than three seconds last night to decide she was his. When he loosened his grip on himself, he realized he wanted her for far longer than a couple days. He wanted her here with him permanently. But that was a topic they'd discuss Monday morning when he dissuaded her from leaving. Because once he claimed her, that was it. She'd be his.

Unaware of his possessive thoughts, Moriah soaped his shoulders and arms, then his torso and stomach. He held his breath, waiting for her to grab his dick, but she didn't. Instead, she knelt before him and washed his feet.

His balls ached watching her from that angle. Her breasts bouncing as she moved higher and scrubbed up and down his legs, his cock brushing against her head during the ministrations. If she noticed — she'd had to notice — she chose to ignore it.

But finally, she looked up at him, and she tentatively grasped his cock. "It's smooth," she murmured as she stroked the length. "But not," she added, tracing the thick veins running along the length. With her other hand she cupped his sac, and he cursed himself a fool for ever agreeing to this. What had he been thinking?

Now, he tried to think of anything and everything that would prevent him from coming on her face or her tits — yeah, that would be a beautiful sight. No! He had to think of something else. Why, oh why, did her lips have to linger so close to the head of his dick?

Moriah allowed the water the fall over his soapy erection and rinse it clean. Then she rubbed the tip along her cheek, as if memorizing the texture. She studied it then lifted her eyes to his and enveloped his hardness with her hot mouth.

He groaned in unison to her as she tasted him. Slowly at first. Back and forth along the shaft. He could feel her tongue swirl along the length. She then released him with an audible pop.

"I've only seen this on the internet," she confessed. "Am I doing it right?"

Straining for control, he nodded. Shrugging, she lifted his cock and licked it underneath, from the base all the way to the tip. Then she sucked it back into her mouth and nearly choked herself on it in an effort to consume all of it.

"Careful," he managed, not wanting her to gag — not this time.

But Moriah ignored him. She took him deep again. And again. And fuck if she didn't suck him like a damn pro.

Just when he couldn't take it anymore, he pulled back.

Chapter Eight

Moriah frowned in disappointment. Why was he stopping her? She was sure she was doing it right if his grunted out sounds of pleasure and his fingers pulling in her hair were any indication.

"What's wrong?" she asked.

"I'm about to come."

She stroked her hand along his length, watching in fascination as beads of pre-cum spilled over his tip. Fighting his grip, she leaned forward and clicked her tongue over it to gather the essence. She hummed in pleasure at the taste.

"Fuck, Moriah."

"Yes, please. Fuck Moriah," she said.

"You have a lot to learn about who's in charge and not trying to take control."

"Was I?"

"You know damn well you were."

She swallowed at his rasped tone and tried to look contrite. She knew his rules. He'd lain them out last night, but she'd thought he was all in with what she'd been doing.

Her head dropped, and she stared at the tile at his feet. Damn it. She didn't want to do something to make him back away from her. Not now when she finally had the opportunity to be with him, not ever. "I'm sorry."

He caught her chin and tilted her face back to look at him. "Hey, don't." His thumb played with her bottom lip. "You didn't know. I didn't give you clear instructions. Now, I'm telling you. I'm not coming, you're not coming again, until I'm inside you. Well, at least until we're in bed and I'm about to take you. Then you might come a few times just to get ready."

"And, um, when do you think this will be?"

"Are you in a hurry?"

Well, you, now that you ask.

82

"I want to be with you as many times as possible this weekend."

"You will be."

"We're going to bed now?"

"No," he laughed and brought her to her feet. He shut off the water and took her hand. "Now, we're getting dressed. Your clothes will be here soon, and you're going to show them off for me?"

Moriah made a face at him as she stumbled after him while guided her out of the shower. Taking one of the soft towels from the warmer, he started rubbing it over her body then dried her hair. He grabbed another from the warmer and flung it around his hips. She stared at the droplets running down his torso to where the towel hung low on his hips. She wanted to lick the little rolling beads of water but knew he wouldn't be pleased with her if she did. Would that earn her a spanking? It would almost be worth it to find out.

Before she could act on the impulse, he drew her toward the vanity and picked up a bottle of lotion. Her eyes widened when she realized it was the light floral fragrance she normally wore.

"That's the kind I use," she said.

83

"Is it?" he asked, but his tone indicated he knew that. Why did he have her scent here? He poured some in his hand then rubbed his palms together briefly before smoothing the cream over her body. He started with her arms, doing each before moving to her shoulders and neck. She let out a half whimper of pleasure as he massaged it in.

He turned her and she closed her eyes as he rubbed more lotion into her back. He moved her legs farther apart with his foot, then she felt him crouch behind her. She knew she was getting wet in a way unrelated to the shower when he worked the fragrance into her legs, his strong hands both rubbing and kneading her muscles. Her stance wobbled when he pressed his mouth to the curve of her ass while he worked, kissing and nibbling at each cheek.

She was one screaming nerve ending by the time his slick hands cupped her rear. He rubbed in the lotion, his fingers teasing her crease, dipping in and making her flinch at the unfamiliar sensation of being touched there.

Then he turned her, but didn't stand from his crouch. His knees hit the floor as he squeezed a little more of the cream into his palms.

"Are you wet?" he asked. His hands skated up her torso, scenting her belly, her ribs, up her sides. When he cupped her breasts, she cried out, her head tilting back and her chest thrusting into him.

"Moriah?" he said, bringing her attention back to his question. "Are you wet?"

"Um-hmm," she whimpered, not changing her stance or looking at him. That seemed to satisfy him. He kneaded the mounds in his hands, pulling and squeezing, working his way out to her aching nipples. He plucked at the taut buds, sending a sizzle of pleasure straight to her core.

"These will look so pretty with clamps on them," he said.

"I thought you said…"

"That I don't have all the paraphernalia? I don't, but I have some tools for your pleasure. Clamps, cuffs, a paddle…some other things. You'll like them."

She doubted she'd like the paddle, but she didn't voice her dissent as he played with her breasts. He could do that all day. No…she'd melt into a puddle long before that.

"Kendrick," she pleaded, unsure what she was asking. She was beginning to shake from his touch all over her. She groaned when his hands left her breasts. But then, she felt his hands skimming down her belly. She felt him sit back. His grip on her hips pulled her closer to him. When she looked down, she saw he was sitting on his heels and he was slouching a little to bring his mouth even with her pussy as she straddled him.

"Oh God," she exclaimed as he parted her and put his mouth on her, licking her intimate flesh.

"Mmm, you are wet," he said. "So wet and sweet."

Her knees buckled and she grabbed at his head as he kept licking, one hand holding her open and the other arm slung around under her ass to hold her up. She shook as her devoured her, her arousal feeding him as he sucked and nipped, drawing his tongue along her slit and gathering all of it.

"Oh God…oh…oh…" she cried, her fingers clenching in his hair as he brought her to the edge of her orgasm. "Kendrick!"

He pulled back, and wiped the back of his hand across his mouth. "Yes?"

"I…you…what…?"

"I said no coming until I had you in my bed."

He had to be fucking kidding. He'd brought her right to the edge and then...

"You bastard," she swore.

He shrugged and stood. "Some might say that." He cupped her cheeks with both hands and leaned in, kissing her lightly. Though she was angry, she responded, tasting herself on his lips.

He lifted her into his arms, carrying her from the bathroom. He gently laid her on the unmade bed and shoved the bedding out of the way. As he knelt over her, caging her in with his arms and legs, she noticed he'd lost his towel somewhere along the way.

"I'll never leave you needy," he said, kissing her again.

"But you..."

"I promised you'd be in my bed."

"Are you going to fuck me?" Though she'd begged him for it, over and over, nerves bombarded her middle and her limbs went cold, something that always happened when she was overwrought whether from something good or bad.

"I had thought I'd wait. I had all kinds of plans for us today." He glanced at the clock beside them. "Your clothes will be delivered in forty-five minutes."

"Plenty of time."

"Not hardly. I want to savor you, take my time—"

"You have been," she argued.

He nipped at her bottom lip. "Trying to be in control again?"

"I just...I want you."

"I want you, too, kitten. I want your little claws digging into my back as you howl with ecstasy. I want your body arching and rubbing against me with a heat you can't control."

A shudder of pleasure racked through her at the pictures he drew for her. "Yes," she simply said, though there'd been no question.

He leaned down and sucked one nipple into his mouth, drawing hard, and she grasped his shoulders, arching just as he'd said. Her legs widened, cradling his hips, and she moaned as he rubbed the length along her. His tip grazed her clit with each drag and made her jerk with little bolts of pleasure.

He was killing her. That's all there was to it. Kendrick just planned to kill her with pleasure. What a way to go.

"Moriah," he whispered, drawing her attention. He didn't speak again until she stared into his eyes. "Are you sure? You need to be absolutely sure."

She smiled softly at him, drawing her thumb along the worry line on his forehead. "I'm sure. You don't understand. I've been sure since I was sixteen and I started thinking of you when I'd lie in bed late at night. You think I couldn't get with a guy in all this time. I went to a private school, but that didn't mean I was sequestered with no male contact. I didn't want anyone but you."

He growled. "But you almost gave it away, almost gave away what's mine!"

"I didn't have a choice," she whispered. She didn't want to remember last night and the fear she'd felt, the sheer terror at the likelihood she'd be raped, because in the end there would have been no way she'd have been willing. But Kendrick had saved her, just as she'd dreamed he always would save her. This one time, he'd be her night and on Monday, she'd start saving herself — and her little sister.

"You have a choice now. You don't have to give your virginity to anyone. You belong to yourself."

"I want you. I want this. Please, Kendrick. Please... You're in charge. I'll do whatever you want. Please..." She was at his mercy, and somehow the begging turned her on—at least, begging him did, because she didn't imagine it would be that way with anyone else. Was this part of what he'd meant by her being submissive to him?

He gave a single nod, and his hands clamped around her wrists, holding them on either side of her head. With a shift, the head of his cock lodged at her entrance. Slowly, he pushed, his fingers clenching around her wrists as he moved into her tightness. She had a fleeting thought of the restraints he'd mentioned, but it was momentary because every bit of her focus was on where he penetrated her.

Beyond her control, her breathing heightened. She shook, staring into Kendrick's molten eyes as he held her enraptured in his gaze. He moved so slowly, so slowly she relaxed, lulled into calm. Then suddenly, he surged forward and she screamed, her body bowing at the flash of pain that seared through her.

"Oh God," she sobbed.

"Shh…shh, shh," he crooned against her lips. His hips stayed still, his invasion complete as his groin pressed flush to hers. His mouth trailed to her ear. "Shh…it's okay, my good little girl. It's all okay. Stay still and get used to me. Feel me owning you, making you all mine."

She clenched around him at that. His thick length did own her. She felt nothing but how his solid girth filled her. So full—so so full and deep.

"I'm yours," she whispered in response.

"Mmm," he growled, his pleasure clear. At least, someone felt good here. Though…the longer they stayed still together, the more she wanted, no *needed* to move. Experimenting, she rolled her hips upward into him and moaned at the sensation that rolled over her. A little pinch of pain. So much pleasure.

"My kitten wants to play?" he asked.

"Yes, please. Please I want to feel it all."

"Oh…you'll get it all," he promised. With that, he pulled back his hips then thrust forward.

"Yes," she cried. "Oh yes." She arched and clawed at him as he started a deep pounding rhythm she couldn't escape, that claimed her as fully as she'd begged to be claimed. It wasn't long before he had her back to the brink of orgasm.

This time he let her go over the edge... No, he shoved her over the edge and he plunged right over with her. His guttural exclamation filling the air and mingling with her screams as they both claimed their release.

Kendrick knelt up, still slowly thrusting as they came down. Her bottom rested on his thighs, her legs drunkenly sprawled out. Her hands moved absently over her torso as the bliss ebbed, heightened then grew again, a muzzy blanket of satisfaction covering her.

He held her open, watching as he moved in and out of her. "So beautiful," he whispered. "So mine."

Dazed, she looked at his cock, seeing their mixed releases, the tinges of her blood along his shaft. She really was his. She blinked up at him, knowing he'd always have part of her, no matter what. "I am," she agreed. "I'm yours, Kendrick."

Chapter Nine

Kendrick moved off of Moriah and kissed his way down her stomach until he reached her mons then removed himself from the bed. He went into his bathroom, retrieved a washcloth, rinsed it under warm water and added a touch of soup then returned to the bedroom.

As carefully as he could, he wiped the blood staining her inner thighs as well as the cum coating her pussy. Fuck, she was beautiful. Beautiful and all his.

He threw the washrag in a trash then held out his arms to help her up. She placed her hands in his, and he lifted her up to her knees and drew her to his chest. "To the shower again." Placing his hands under her ass, he lifted her. She wrapped her legs around his hips.

This time around, the shower was a more practical affair. He finished quickly, soaped her up then left her to enjoy the water while he dressed.

By the time she exited the bathroom in a fluffy towel, the fashion designer had come and gone, and Kendrick had lain out three outfits on the bed for her to choose from, including appropriate shoes and undergarments. He'd put some more casual garments in the closet since he wanted her to choose from these, his favorites of the delivery. It didn't take much imagination to realized he'd really like wrapping Moriah in the best of everything, be it clothes, jewelry or his arms.

"What's this?" she asked with a smile.

"Clothes for you. I'd like to take you to lunch and maybe out for the afternoon."

Moriah perused the outfits. "I love this cute black dress with the nude sandals, but...there's no underwear for it here. Or strapless bra."

Kendrick smirked. "According to the designer, this dress is meant to be worn without a bra or panties. I think you made a good choice," he added and gathered up the other outfits. "You'll make that dress look amazing."

"Wait," she called softly has he took the remaining clothing to his closet. "I didn't pick yet."

"You did," he assured her. "You said you loved it."

"I did before I found out there were no undergarments for it."

"That's not a reason not to love it and wear it. You don't need the bra and panties."

With a grimace or frustration, she dropped the towel then slid the dress on and wandered over to a mirror. "Oh Lord, my nipples are peeking out through the fabric. I can't wear this."

"You can, and you will," he declared. He came up behind her and wrapped his arms around her torso. He put his head on her bare shoulder. "You look beautiful."

She blushed and lowered her gaze. "Fine. I'll wear it for you."

"Thank you," he murmured then turned her around.

"Goodness, no underwear… Let's just hope I don't spot or anything."

It hadn't occurred to him she might need the barrier of underwear because of their lovemaking. "If you really want, you can wear one of the other outfits. I want you to be comfortable."

"It's fine," she sighed. She placed her arms around his neck and leaned into him, inviting him for a kiss. And yes, he felt her nipples through the material. She didn't need a bra though. Her breasts were perfect.

He kissed her then, long and passionate. "Are you tender?" he asked between kisses.

"I'm okay," she responded. "The pleasure was worth the pain."

He released her and spanked her ass to move her along to the living room. "Let's go then."

* * * *

Kendrick had his security/driver drop him and Moriah off at his favorite restaurant. It was a small Italian place—quiet, a hidden gem really. The food was amazing.

The host quickly seated them in a quiet corner of an outside garden patio. With the lovely weather, it was truly the perfect place for his first intimate outing with Moriah. The server came and filled their glasses with water and table wine while Kendrick pulled out the chair for his sexy woman.

Once seated, they made small talk about the mild weather while they perused the menu. However, before they could order, an unexpected — and highly unwanted — guest joined them.

Jofre placed his hand upon Moriah's shoulder and squeezed it hard as he kissed the top of her head in greeting.

"Hey, sweetie," he said, so saccharine sweet it left a bad taste in Kendrick's mouth. Then Jof pulled over a chair and sat at the table with them.

"How are my two favorite people?" Jof asked. "Having a good time?"

It took everything in Kendrick not the punch the guy. Moriah's demeanor changed, as well. She sipped her wine and refused to look up from her empty plate. She seemed hunched in on herself, something he hated and never wanted to see again.

"What are you doing here?" Kendrick growled.

"I'm checking up on my daughter. I take it all went well with the...deflowering?"

Moriah choked into her wine.

"How did you know where to find us?" Kendrick asked, refusing to address her father's tasteless comment. Nothing that happened between Kendrick and Moriah was any of the man's business, parent or not. He put his hand in the air, which prompted his security to come over. Yes, he lived in the same city as Jof, but it unsettled Kendrick that the man had tracked them here.

"I have my ways."

The son of a bitch must still have friends at the firm—unfortunately in the same building where Kendrick lived. Well, he'd rectify this problem soon enough.

Jof looked surprised and uncomfortable as Kendrick's guard came over. Kendrick suppressed a smile. Jof was quite familiar with Frank from the day Jof had been thrown out of Kendrick's office building. Frank, very large and very much in charge when required to be, was the head of his security team.

"Take Moriah to place a to-go order for both of us then get the car. I'll follow shortly—after I take care of some...business."

98

Moriah didn't object when Frank helped her from her chair and led her away. Kendrick watched her go. She nervously glanced over her shoulder as she went. When she was out of sight, he turned his attention to their uninvited guest.

"Aw," Jof smirked. "I know that look. You two in love already, Ken?"

Kendrick leveled a stare at him. "Again. Why are you here?"

"I told you. I'm checking up on my daughter."

"You're trying to intimidate her."

"Well, I'm worried you aren't taking proper care of her—might be filling her head with nonsense. I just want her to know Daddy is always watching."

"You're a sick bastard."

"Well, you were just supposed to just fill her pussy, not her head. I want to remind her where her loyalties lay… Or do you plan to propose? That's a deal we can work out right now, if you wish."

As if he'd let this fucker come anywhere near his union with Moriah. From here on, Kendrick intended to keep her as far from the man as possible, with zero contact if he had his way.

"If we marry, you'll have no part in it."

"Ah. So it's crossed your mind."

"Fuck off."

Jof tsked. "Am I getting to you? This is why the board kept me around. I'm the better businessman. You take things too personally, and you don't have the balls to do what needs to be done."

"They won't keep you much longer since I'm telling them about your embezzlement."

"I've replaced that money already. Just a misunderstanding is all."

"Not possible." The money was in Moriah's bank account, not Jof's. He'd been very clear about that going into this arrangement. And even if it had gone into Jof's account, a transfer of that amount couldn't have been completed already.

"No? Did you really think I wouldn't have access to Moriah's bank account? I had my dear daughter sign a power of attorney when she turned eighteen. She is nothing without me, and she knows it. And she will be very distraught if you put her dear Daddy in jail, so be a good future son-in-law and let it go."

Fuck. He'd need to call his lawyers the moment he was away from Jof. Until then, he'd have to play the game. He'd talk to Moriah, as well. It was time for a serious conversation.

Kendrick rose from his seat and threw down some cash and walked away.

"No goodbye?" Jof laughed. "Hope your hand is feeling better."

As Kendrick made his way out, he stopped by the front. Bless the chef who'd prepared everything immediately and had the order ready for him. He took the picnic basket, thanked the staff, and went outside to where his car waited.

Poor Moriah looked so sad as he got into the backseat.

"I'm so sorry," she rushed.

Kendrick held up his hand. "Do not apologize for things that aren't your fault."

She offered him a half smile then looked out the window. As he texted his finance team to confirm what Jof said, he spoke to Frank. "Are you up to flying today?"

"Sure thing, Boss."

"Let's go back to the office then. We'll take the helicopter to my little hideaway." Kendrick didn't want to say where, so it would be a surprise for Moriah. But he knew she'd love it, and it was a great place for a picnic.

"I have never been in a helicopter," Moriah said.

"Well, you're in good hands with Frank. He flew helicopters for special op missions during Operation Iraqi Freedom."

It didn't take long to get to the helipad on the roof of the building. And Kendrick found himself immensely enjoying the experience again through Moriah's eyes. She seemed so excited to be in a helicopter.

"The city is so beautiful from up here," she said into her headset.

Kendrick nodded, his eyes on her gleaming hair and wide smile rather than on the skyline she gushed over.

"Where are we going?" she asked.

"For a picnic." He motioned toward the picnic basket.

She laughed. "But where?"

"It's a surprise." He winked at her.

Chapter Ten

Moriah wanted to enjoy this day, but first, she wanted to know what had happened between Kendrick and her father. With the questions ricocheting around her head, she knew she'd be distracted and not enjoy the picnic as much as she should—and she wanted every bit of enjoyment she could with Kendrick. She'd wanted him for so long and would only have him for just a blip of time.

She couldn't believe her father. She couldn't believe what he'd said or that he'd shown up at the restaurant, acting as if everything was just peachy.

"What happened with my dad?" she asked.

"You don't want to talk about that," Kendrick said, squeezing her hand.

"No, I really do. I want to get it out of the way so we can enjoy the rest of our day." Or at least so they could try. Tension vibrated off Kendrick. Whatever Jofre had said, it wasn't pleasant.

Kendrick sighed then jerked a nod.

"Frank," he said into the headset. "Can you change our channel back here, so we can have a private conversation?"

"Sure thing, Boss."

Kendrick didn't speak until a faint change in the air sound signaled the change of frequency. "When I told him I was pressing charges, he said he'd already replaced the money he'd stolen."

"How?" she exclaimed. Her father didn't have that sort of cash. God knew what he'd done with what he'd taken from Kendrick's company.

"He claimed it was from your bank account, that you gave him power of attorney and, thereby, access to the funds."

"I did not! No. I never have! I don't trust him that much—not since what he did to my mother. He was…despicable. Besides, until yesterday, I had nothing for him to manage. There would have been no reason to give him that sort of access."

Kendrick nodded again and pulled out his phone, already texting while he spoke. "So he's bluffing."

"He has to be." Gnawing anger hollowed her belly, and she thought she might be sick. If he'd stolen from her…

And it would be theft. She'd already decided she wasn't giving him the money, not a penny. He could rot in jail. Somehow, she'd figure out a way to get Jade, to save her. With the money from Kendrick she could.

"Is it possible to check my account?" she asked. "To block him. He can't do this…" Tears burned in her eyes.

"Moriah," he murmured. He slid the phone into his suit pocket and reached for her hand. His thumb smoothed back and forth over the top of her fingers. "It's okay. I'll make sure of it."

"It's not. It's not! He can't do this. He can't… What he did…that's trafficking, right? Taking my money like he's some sort of pimp?"

"You agreed."

"That doesn't make it legal. It's still a form of sex trade and illegal in most places."

"That's probably why he did it on a private island. If you hate him so much and don't trust him, why did you agree?"

There was no reason to keep it a secret. Kendrick seemed to know most everything about her.

"He coerced me and gave me no other choice. My sister —"

"Your sister?" he interrupted. "How did I not know you have a sister? I've made it my business to know just about everything about him."

"She's six. She's been shielded more than I ever was. He doesn't have wealth rivaling yours, but he has enough that there were vague threats against me from the time I was born. Kidnapping and such. I guess it worried him enough that after Jade was born, he's basically kept her hidden. Not that I think he really loves her, but I don't know what his end game is."

A muscle ticked in Kendrick's cheek though the rest of his expression remained impassive. "And?" he asked.

"And if I didn't do what he wanted, he threatened to send my sister away to live with her drug-addicted birth mom. That woman hates Jade and only had her because my dad paid her not to terminate the pregnancy. She signed away her rights the day Jade was born. For a while, I thought he loved the baby. Now, I think she was just another pawn. When he pressured me into agreeing to sell my virginity, I was scared for her. I *am* scared for her. I can't even comprehend what he might do. The only reason I said I'd go through with the auction was to protect her. Once I had the money, once the weekend was over, I planned to find a way to take her away. Somewhere. Anywhere away from him." Moriah knew that smacked of abduction, but she'd do anything to make sure Jade was safe, even sell herself.

Kendrick had started texting again while she spoke.

"What are you doing?" she asked, unable to hold back her annoyance.

"Taking care of business."

"What?" she exclaimed. She'd poured out her heart, and he was doing business?

"Our business," he clarified. "I'm dealing with the finances — yours and mine — and setting up an appointment with the cops. Probably tomorrow afternoon. I'm also having my assistant arrange a meeting with my friend, Senator McKenzie. She'll help to make sure Jof goes down, though she'll be discreet and keep it out of the public eye. She can also smooth the way for custody of your sister. Parental rights were signed over and he's going to prison. You're her closest relative and willing to take her, so Jade should be placed in your provisional care."

"Oh…" She hadn't imagined he could do that. "You can do that?"

"Another hefty campaign donation will ease the way, but yes, I can."

"Is that legal?"

"More legal than anything your father has done lately."

The phone lit up in his hand, and he glanced down at it then grinned. "Good," he enthused. "The money is still in your account, and we've gotten the assets frozen for the time being."

"How long?" His deposit aside, she'd need her savings to live come Monday. "And how did you get access to my account?"

He raised a brow at her as if to ask if that were really a question. "Moriah, you're my business, which makes everything about you my business, too. Before I even set foot at that auction, I had my people obtain any info I thought I'd need. And one of my colleagues has some, let's say, *resources* at his disposal."

"Resources? Do you mean hackers?"

"I'm fairly sure Chase—that's my friend—prefers not to call them that. But..." He tipped his head from one side and then to the other. "Probably. I don't ask. I just make sure my own assets are well protected. The final peg in that gate is *Berg Trade Financial*."

She nodded, listening. *Berg Trade* was the branch Jofre worked for as a VP, but she knew little about all of Kendrick's businesses.

"*Bergana Holdings*, the umbrella company—*my* company—owns a plethora of businesses. *Berg Trade* is the only portion ruled by a board of directors. That was my father's failing and why I've never allowed anyone to dictate how I run my companies. I'm not happy with the structure at *Berg Trade*, but I'm unwilling to let it go. It was my work that made it into the powerhouse financial institution it is today. When I inherited my dad's shares, I started the undertaking of wresting back full power, so I

111

don't have to answer to a fucking board of directors. Though I'm pissed as hell at Jofre for stealing from me, he's given me exactly what I need to take them down and get back my company."

"So then you can do anything you want?"

"Well," he laughed, "no. There are still plenty of checks and balances in place to be sure everything stays lawful and nobody's getting swindled. Even multi-billionaires endure plenty of governmental oversights and audits for their businesses. Things can be concealed, but frankly, I don't have that kind of time."

She stared at him, unsure what to say. Kendrick was so much more than she'd imagined. She'd known he was rich, but not that he own multiple businesses. "So…what my father stole from you was basically pennies?"

"Yes. But a small leak only gets bigger — and nobody steals from me and gets away with it."

She swallowed, feeling forewarned even though thievery wasn't in her personality. "And what you bid on me? Also pennies."

He glanced up at Frank, as if to ensure he wasn't listening, then looked back at her. "I would have bid everything for you."

Her lips parted, breathing suddenly hard.

He pulled her hand toward him and turned it palm up. His finger traced along her sensitive skin. *M. I. N. E*, he wrote. Then he closed her fingers around it and looked up at her, his gaze tender before his mouth twisted into a playful smirk. She squirmed, the resulting heat from his gaze reminding her she wasn't wearing panties and was completely bare for him.

"I'll remind you how much in a few minutes," he promised.

"We're almost there?" she asked, looking out the window. She'd been so engrossed with speaking with him, she hadn't been paying attention.

"Almost," he confirmed.

Peering about, she saw they'd left the city far behind and were closing in on a large estate, the only structure she saw for miles.

"Yours?" she asked.

"From my grandparents. We won't be going in. It's been locked up for over twenty-five years and needs massive structural work. I want to tear it down, but the local historical society is blocking me."

113

"It does look like pretty old architecture," she said as the copter got closer to the ground. "So...why are we here if we're not going in?"

"I keep the grounds maintained, and they're private. If you look this way," he directed her gaze out his window, "you'll see the gazebo and a guesthouse. I thought we could picnic there beside the stream."

Sure enough, she saw the small bungalow-style house, and about a hundred feet from it, across a stretch of manicured lawn, was a white, octagonal shelter beside a flow of rushing water.

"It's beautiful," she said.

"I come here to think sometimes. To get away from all the noise," he told her as the helicopter set down gently. As if on cue, the engines cut, plunging them into near silence—at least much closer to it. Kendrick helped her out of her headphones and belt then guided her out and grabbed their picnic basket. He glanced at his watch before turning to Frank, who'd jumped down beside them. "Come back in three hours."

"With all due respect, sir, I'd rather not," he replied. "I need to do a sweep of the grounds then I'll give you complete privacy."

She looked at Kendrick for his reaction. She understood the need for security, especially for someone in his position. God knew she'd dealt with having a detail watch her most of her life, and her father had far lesser wealth. However, she was curious how Kendrick would take the opposition to his dictate.

He merely nodded. "Very well," he replied. "You're correct. We can't take chances with Moriah's safety."

"Or yours," she exclaimed.

"I would be fine." He shook his head as if that weren't a worry while Frank appeared faintly amused. "We'll be at the gazebo," he told his guard. His hand planted at the small of Moriah's back as he guided her away. "We'll head to the guesthouse after we eat."

"Very well, sir," Frank replied. "I'll make sure it's secure then leave you to your privacy."

But Moriah got the feeling he wouldn't be very far from them, even when out of sight. The thought was fleeting, though. Her awareness was centered on the tingles emanating from the light touch of Kendrick's fingers just above her ass. Excitement fluttered through her, stronger today, now that she knew what it was to belong to him, how it would feel for him to shift his palm scant inches lower to cup her behind.

His lips brushed her ear as they walked. "How are you feeling today? Sore?"

Maybe a little but if that would stop him from touching her... "Not really," she hedged.

"Good," he whispered, despite there being no one around to hear. Shivers skated down her spine at his dark, sensual tone. "After I feed you, I want to be deep inside you again. Maybe, you'd like to ride me today."

She swallowed and nervously ran her tongue over her lips. "Maybe," she echoed, the sound barely more than a breathy gasp. "I'm not sure...how..."

"Trust me, I'll guide you. Every step of the way."

"Okay. Yes, I'd like that. I think—no, I know—I'd like to suck your cock again," she admitted, heat rushing to her cheeks at her declaration.

"So shy yet so bold. Such an intriguing mix, kitten."

"I just want as much of you as possible this weekend."

He tensed beside her at the reminder of their circumstance. "You can have as much of me as you want, whenever you want," he replied. "I certainly intend to take as much of you as *I* want. And trust me, that desire is boundless."

His hand skimmed down to finally cup her ass. "No more mention of that fucking auction or time limits," he growled. "It's just you and me and this moment and getting all the pleasure we can."

"But—"

"Are you asking for a spanking, Moriah?" he asked, interrupting her protest when she would have confessed she couldn't get the expiration date off her mind.

"Um…" Was she? Several times, he'd threatened to put her over his knee, but so far, had never delivered. Maybe, she hadn't pushed him enough. Maybe, it was just words, idle threats…sex talk.

Rather than answer, she shrugged.

"Oh, little girl, you have no idea who you're provoking."

Chapter Eleven

Breaking from his light embrace, she ran ahead of him then skipped up the stairs into the latticed gazebo. Benches lined the edges, and when Kendrick joined her, he lifted one of the seats to reveal a storage area and withdrew a thick blanket. He spread it out on the wood-planked floor and put their basket on one side of it. Sitting with his legs in front of him, he reached for her and pulled her into his lap to straddle him.

"When you run like that, I get to see tantalizing glimpses of that ass I'm going redden later," he growled, slipping his hands beneath her skirt to cup said ass.

With nothing covering her sex, her tender folds were pushed up against the solid ridge in his pants. She groaned at the sensation of it pressing into her. Her eyes closed, and her head dropped back as she rocked her hips.

"Not here, Moriah," Kendrick warned as he kissed her neck.

"It feels…good," she moaned, thinking perhaps she could get off on the sensations spiraling through her.

"Moriah. No," he rasped. His hands tightened on her hips, keeping her still. "Not where anyone can see or hear what's only mine."

"There's no one—"

"There's Frank, and I don't want to fucking fire him because he witnesses you getting off."

She pressed harder into him, fighting his grip. "I'll be quiet."

"No," he replied and swiftly lifted her off him and plopped her onto the blanket beside him. "You're eating lunch, then I'm taking you inside and giving you the spanking you so sorely deserve. Then I'm going to fuck you hard—and maybe, I'll let you come if you're a good girl."

"I'll be good."

He raised an eyebrow at her, obviously refuting her claim.

Her hands clasped in her lap, and she stared at her pale fingernails. She kind of hated it the polish on them. She liked bold colors. She'd left behind spankings and little girl things in her childhood — not that she'd actually been spanked after the age of ten. By that age, Jof was more into emotional discipline or more accurately, emotional manipulation and verbal abuse.

"I don't want a spanking," she whispered.

"Yes, you do." Kendrick opened the basket as if they weren't discussing anything more innocuous than the weather. He pulled out two plates — real china plates, not the paper or plastic one would expect — and started dishing up their meal. He handed her hers along with her utensils then poured them both glasses of sparkling water.

"No, really, I don't," she argued.

"Eat," was all he said.

"You're so bossy." But she took a bite of the delicious pasta on her plate and barely suppressed a moan at the flavors. She took another, thinking perhaps it was the best she'd ever had.

He shrugged. "You'll get used to it."

"Well, at least, you can't boss me around after tomorrow night."

His fingers whitened around the fork he held, before he dropped it on his plate. Oops. He'd told her not to mention that. His plate clattered to the blanket. She protested as he took hers and set it beside his dish. Before she knew what was happening, he was up and she was over his shoulder. One of his arms locked her legs in place while the other crossed higher and held down her dress.

"Put me down," she screeched as he marched down the steps and across the yard toward the small guesthouse.

"No fucking way."

Frank was coming out of the house as Kendrick approached.

"Secure?" Kendrick asked.

"Yes, sir."

"Good." He headed for the door.

"Frank, help me!" she yelled, smacking Kendrick's back. The guard shook his head, smiling, and walked away toward the crumbling main house. "Frank!"

He ignored her, showing her exactly where his loyalty lay. In his wallet. Kendrick paid him;

therefore, Kendrick could do whatever he wanted and Frank would look the other way.

She hit Kendrick's back harder as he stormed inside. "Put me down, you bastard! Put me down!"

"As you wish." He dropped her on a bed, and she pounced before she tried to scramble away. He was over her in an instant, caging her in place. She shoved against him, but he didn't give her an inch. Instead, one of his arms came around her, pulling her tighter to him. Then he knelt up and dragged her along with him. Taking advantage of the movement, she twisted away, shoving her knee into his stomach in the process. He caught her around the waist as she dove away. She landed over his lap with an oomph!

"Let me up!" she screamed as he shoved up her skirt, baring her ass. His hand connected with one cheek, and Moriah shrieked in outrage, twisting and beating on his leg, the only part of him she could get to with him as she lay over his parted thighs, one of his arms pinned across her back. The more she struggled the more his palm rained down on her poor behind.

"I warned you, kitten," he said calmly. "Though, maybe, I should call you hellcat. I have to tell you, baby, you're turning me on. I might need to spank you often."

"Let me go," she whined. Heat and pain radiated across her lower half. Tears poured down her cheeks. "I hate you," she whispered, feeling completely humiliated that he'd do this to her.

"No, you don't. Just feel, and you'll see you don't hate it — or me — as much as you think."

She shook her head, denying what she already felt. "Stop."

But he didn't. The thwacks continued in a steady rhythm. The fire licking at her pussy in a completely disturbing way. It took long moments before she realized she'd stopped protesting and was actually moaning, anticipating each spank of his hand on her needy behind. What the hell? How was that possible? She'd read about it, but never believed it.

"Kendrick," she moaned, afraid of what was happening, what he was bringing out of her.

"You feel it?"

"Yes," she choked. "Kendrick, I—"

"Just let it happen," he coaxed, pausing momentarily.

She groaned in protest then his fingers stroked over her pussy and her eyes rolled back, the tight tension in her core ratcheting even higher. Her breasts were so achy, the nipples so tight, she could barely stand the rub against his pantleg. Each brush sent pleasured torture straight to her core.

"Fuck, you're so wet," he murmured. "I think a few more and you'll be there."

"Be where?" she exclaimed. "Kendrick, I need—"

She cried out as he spanked her again. The pleasure-pain exploded across her skin, followed by another then another, and Moriah lost touch with the moment, feeling herself flying as she plummeted over the edge of sanity. The climax was unlike anything she'd experienced last night or on her own.

When she regained herself, she was on her back, her legs bent around his hips. He'd shoved his pants to his thighs and surged hard into her in an unrelenting rhythm. He wrenched aside of the top of her dress and captured her nipple in his mouth, sucking with the same fervor as he fucked her pussy. It was wild and urgent, holding nothing back. Kendrick was claiming her, taking her, making it clear she was his.

"Don't ever mention leaving me," he growled, never halting his pumping. "Never. You're mine. Mine, Moriah!"

"Yes," she cried, arching beneath him, her sex clenching around his thick, driving shaft.

"Say it," he demanded. "Tell me you're mine."

"I'm yours," she screamed.

"That's right. Mine. You're mine. Now, come around my cock, kitten. Take all of my seed from me. Take it all in you, and show me you're mine. Oh," he groaned as her body immediately clamped down at his words. She couldn't help it. His demands, his dirty talk pulled her right over to the dark side, and she'd do anything he wanted. She was helpless to it. "Yeah, that's right," he growled. Clench around me. Take it all from me. Milk my cock, Moriah. Show me who this pussy belongs to."

She arched beneath him on a loud cry, her body exploding into another orgasm that rolled through her, ebbing then growing, bigger and bigger, stealing her breath then her sight. She heard Kendrick groan from deep in his soul, the sound vibrating into her.

She wondered what he meant…why he sounded like he wasn't ever letting her go, but as

126

she drifted away, she didn't care about anything but being with him and being his. Maybe, it was pillow talk. Maybe, it was a lot more.

Later…she'd ask…later…

When her vision cleared, Kendrick was still over her, he was still lodged deep inside her body. He stared down into her eyes.

"You passed out."

"Did I?" she whispered, her voice hoarse.

He nodded, looking smug. "Can't say I've ever had that happen before."

She didn't want to think of anyone before or after her. She glanced away, the movement — or even just breathing, actually — emphasizing what he'd done to her body since dragging her into the house. In that, she had no complaints. She'd revel in the sensual ache as long as it lasted.

"Well," she sniped. "It was probably from lack of sustenance. You've barely let me eat since I've been with you. I probably fainted from weakness."

"Uh-huh," he said dryly. "Tell me all about that story. My palm is itching for another round."

"Oh God," she gasped. Her body clenched at the thought, but she confessed, "I don't think I could do another round."

He smiled tenderly. "Actually, I don't think you could either. I'm not so much of a sadist that I'd try. But...I'm not opposed to putting my mouthy girl in the corner."

Her mouth opened and closed like a fish out of water. "You...do that?"

"Never have before, but with you, I just might."

"Uh..." The sound was mostly a whimper.

He chuckled. "First, let's feed you."

They both groaned as he pulled free. He righted his clothes, and she sat up, swinging her legs to the edge of the bed. "I should go—"

He cut her off with a shake of his head. "I like you smelling like me." He leaned in and dragged his nose along her neck. "Feeling me still in you, feeling me filling you," he rumbled. "Feeling owned by me."

He pulled her to her feet beside him, and she felt every bit of what he'd said. Filled and completely owned by him.

Chapter Twelve

Back at their picnic on the gazebo, Moriah looked into his eyes adoringly as he brought the spoon to her mouth, giving her the last bite of their dessert. It was a simple lemon tart of sorts, rich and delicate, and perfect to share. She chewed slowly and savored the sweet and sour before she swallowed, all without breaking their gaze. Her eyes sparkled with unspoken words. She probably didn't realize she was revealing so much with her regard, but he was old enough to recognize the sentiments that lingered in those beautiful depths.

Kendrick leaned in and lick a little bit of whipped lemon off the corner of her mouth. However, he couldn't stop there. That little taste turned into a full-blown kiss. Slow, passionate, exploring. His tongue swept in to possess her.

When they separated, panting, their lips hovered only a hairsbreadth apart, both waiting in expectation. Would they fall into each other again?

She inhaled softly as if to mark a memory, to capture his scent maybe, then gently brushed her nose against his before she leaned her forehead to his. While this might have come off as a simple display of affection to others, Kendrick read her body language as declarations of how much she trusted him and how much she welcomed him into her space.

He was humbled by Moriah's confidence in him. A lesser man might have been intimidated, might have been concerned by the speed in which the relationship was evolving, but not Kendrick. There was no need to overanalyze what they had. Taking risks and coming out on top was a day-to-day norm for him. Why would he doubt his instincts now?

Kendrick noted it would be easy for him to become obsessed with Moriah. He'd always had a dominant personality, and as a natural leader, that made him want to take charge of things, to be in control, and get his way. These character traits made him very successful in life. Moriah's personality fit with his in the way two matching puzzle pieces snap together into place. She was perfect for him. She seemed almost eager to please him, craved his guidance, and deferred to him in things of importance, while still being able to maintain her strong spirit—that latter was extremely important to him. He didn't want a puppet, that's for sure. Best of all, she was brilliant, interesting to converse with, easy to like, and fun to be around. And though she might not realize it yet, he wasn't letting her go come Monday.

She'd said she was his, she gave herself to him, and he was holding her to everything she'd promised. *"Yes, I'll obey you."* … *"I'm yours, Kendrick."* …

Moriah pulled back and smiled at him, drawing him from his musings. "What are you thinking about?"

In the soft, late-afternoon light, her hair blowing in the breeze, her cheeks radiating a satisfied glow from their intimacy, and her lips pink and swollen from his kiss, he almost wished he'd hired a photographer for the day. He could imagine wonderful photos of her on his walls.

"Nothing of concern," he responded with a wink. "Just noting how beautiful you are."

She giggled and dropped her gaze, blushing at the compliment, and his heart melted. Fuck. Jof was right. He was already in love with everything Moriah. He wanted to love her, protect her, give her the best of all he had, and cherish her.

"Why do you keep looking at me like that?"

"I told you," he said. "You're beautiful."

"It's more than that," she whispered then gazed off into the distance. "Your eyes...they...I don't know. They devour me."

Kendrick chuckled. "Wow. That sounds sinister."

She laughed then, too. "Right?" She rose from the blanket. "You're so intense, is all."

"Is that a bad thing?" he asked as he climbed to his feet. He captured her in his arms. "I don't want to scare you off."

Moriah shook her head. "No. And you could never scare me off. You own me, remember? I'm yours."

He smacked her ass for her sassy rebuttal. "Don't you forget it."

"Can we take a walk?"

"Well, there's a hedge labyrinth behind the main house. Would you like to see it?"

"Really" She damn near bounced in excitement. "Yes!"

"The gardens are one of the things I make sure are kept up on property. I sometimes host charity events on the patio when the weather is nice like this."

"What's in the middle?"

He laughed. "You'll have to wait and see!"

Taking his hand in hers, Moriah pulled him toward the back of the property. He couldn't help but get excited with her. She was so full of life, and in that moment, he realized he'd become a jaded asshole. He rarely enjoyed these things anymore—helicopter rides and such. But with Moriah, it suddenly all seemed new and interesting.

"How fun!" She giggled as she navigated the stone pathway, dragging him along in her haste to get through the immaculately hedged labyrinth. "This is so awesome!" she exclaimed in breathless anticipation.

He chuckled at her childlike wonder and was glad he'd sought the best gardeners and landscapers in the area to maintain the back garden. The hedges were healthy — tall and thick enough to well-hide the surprise in the middle, making for an exciting journey even though the labyrinth didn't have the navigational challenges of a maze.

When they finally reached the center, Moriah inhaled sharply. Releasing his hand, she took tentative steps toward the old marble fountain. "It's amazing. The water is so clean and clear." She circled the water feature to gander at the many statues of Greek deities positioned around the blooming garden.

Kendrick sat on the large stone bench, content to watch his kitten explore and play — and play she did. To his surprise, she kicked off her shoes and actually got into the fountain.

"You should come wade with me," she called over her shoulder. "The water is wonderful."

He shook his head. "You enjoy. I like watching."

"Do you now? You like to watch?" He knew she was about to do something absolutely naughty because her lips curved up in a mischievous smile. "Okay. Watch this then." She took off her dress and tossed it onto the ground, leaving her standing in the fountain as naked as the marble nymphs dancing around them.

"Moriah!" he snapped and shot to his feet.

"What?" she laughed. "No one is around. And see, now you're coming over here. Anyway, I've never been skinny-dipping, and I've always wanted to try it."

Kendrick rolled his eyes. "That's a fountain. You don't swim in fountains. If you want to go skinny-dipping, then someday, I'll take you somewhere you can do so." He held out his hand to help her step out, but she didn't take it.

Moriah crossed her arms and pouted. "I don't want to get out yet." Then she kicked her foot and splashed him. She laughed and lunged away from his grasp, escaping his clutches and retreating farther into the fountain.

He rubbed the drops of water from his face with as much dignity as he could, considering the absurd situation. "I obviously didn't spank you enough earlier."

"You did," she assured. She marched around the fountain one last time before hopping out. She sashayed over to him before wrapping her arms around his neck and crushing her bare body against his. "I'm being bad. I'm sorry. Do you forgive me?"

How could he not when she asked so sweetly? "I'm still going to spank you when we get home." His palms cupped her bare rear.

"I wouldn't expect anything less." She pulled her arms down and flounced over to the stone bench. "Let's just get it over with. I'd rather not wait."

"Excuse me?"

She bent over, grasped the edge of the seat and swayed her ass at him. "Come on now. Just do it already."

Little brat. "What happened to Miss 'I don't think I could do another round'?"

Moriah shrugged. "That was a couple hours ago. I'm fine now. I can hardly tell you even spanked me." She looked over her shoulder and lifted her brows. "You must be out of practice. Pity."

Kendrick moved to where she was, nudged her aside and sat himself on the bench. In rapid succession, snatched her wrist, pulled her over his lap, adjusted her to a safe prone position to receive discipline, and immediately started dishing that discipline out.

It happened so fast all Moriah could do was let out a small squeak in protest, but by then, his palm was already reddening her rear something fierce—much harder than he'd done previously, lest she ever make the mistake of taunting him again with "I can hardly tell you ever spanked me. You must be out of practice."

When she screamed in objection, he smacked her ass even harder. "Quiet. Be quiet, Moriah. Right now." She instantly fell silent. Other than for her gasping, she did as he instructed. And while he spanked the little brat, he listed his reasons for doing so, with extra emphasis on her sudden change in attitude.

"It's called topping from the bottom. Have you ever heard of that?"

"No," she sobbed.

He quickly pulled her off his lap and positioned her so she straddled his legs with her weight resting on her thighs rather than her burning rear. He tsked and wiped the tears from her cheeks with the pads of his thumbs.

"Moriah. It means you're trying to control the relationship after you've assigned that control to someone else. Do you remember what you agreed to on the plane?"

She sniffled. "I agreed to obey you."

137

"Exactly."

"In the bedroom," she added, lowering her gaze. "We're not in a bedroom."

"You're naked. This counts as bedroom play."

"Are we going to have sex then?"

Damn. She sounded almost hopeful. She still had a lot to learn, he acknowledged, and he didn't want to ruin the day. "Would you like that, kitten?"

She lifted an unsure shoulder. "Maybe."

Kendrick decided his cock needed a spanking for getting fucking hard from her simple *maybe*. "I'll tell you what. If you want it, you're free to proceed. Pull down the zipper and see how much I want you right now."

Moriah looked down between her legs to the bulge resting between his. Obviously intrigued, she rose and, after unzipping his pants, pulled his rigid cock from the fabric constraints.

"What now?" she asked, licking her lips.

"Well, what do you want to do?" he asked.

Rather than answering, she lowered herself to her knees and wrapped her mouth around him. Kendrick couldn't have imagined how sexy it would be to have Moriah naked and on her knees, sucking his dick in the center of a garden in the middle of the afternoon.

He groaned as she sucked and licked until he was on the edge of coming. Perhaps sensing how close he was, she got to her feet and, with measured movements, straddled him again. On her tippy-toes, she fisted his shaft and guided the moist head to her pussy.

"That's it, kitten. Nice and slow. Take your time."

She carefully impaled herself, slowly lowering herself upon his girth with moans of pain and pleasure. By the time she was fully seated, she was panting and her fingernails dug into his shoulders.

His eyes almost rolled back at the sensation of her silky heat enveloping him. Her walls squeezed him as her own reactions rolled through her, but he didn't rush her. He let her get used to the new position, the width and length of his dick so deep inside her pussy.

"Now what?" she whispered.

He kissed her neck, grappling with his control, when every instinct told him to take over. "I recommend moving your hips gently."

Moriah complied, rocking back and forth. It must have felt as good to her as it did to him because she increased her speed. She soon found her rhythm and rode him like a pro, yelping her passion as she sought her climax.

It didn't take long. She came, her warm, tight pussy gripping his dick like a vise as she fucked him quick and hard. Tingles clawed at the base of his spine, beckoning him to let go. He wanted her to reach her release first. Finally, she threw back her head and screamed her climax, propelling him to spill within her.

When they both came back to themselves, Moriah was content to lay her head on his shoulder and rest. His arms closed around her. He never wanted to let her go. He never would! That knowledge echoed through him, calming him.

They stayed like that for a while, him simply holding her, until the distant *womp-womp-womp* sound roused him from his stupor.

He needed to get Moriah up and dressed. "Up you go, kitten."

* * * *

While Kendrick knew Moriah's ass was sore, as was everything below her waist considering all the sex they'd enjoyed that day, his kitten didn't show any discomfort—at least, not at the moment. To allow time for his assistant and chef to prepare for the seven o'clock surprise at home, he'd had Frank take them on a helicopter tour of the city. Moriah was entranced.

"It's so beautiful from up here," she marveled.

Kendrick nodded, though his sights were on her, not the cityscape. He could watch her forever.

"Will you take me to church in the morning?" she asked, pointing to a large cathedral.

"Of course."

She beamed. "My dad would never take me. I'd either have to go alone, or not go at all."

"Well, I'm nothing like your father," he assured. His phone buzzed. It was his assistant.

Dinner ready. Flowers, as requested. Bath drawn. Fireplace lit.

He texted his thanks and instructed Frank to take them home.

141

Chapter Thirteen

Not ten minutes after Kendrick instructed Frank to bring them to the penthouse, Moriah and Kendrick were walking through the door. She immediately sensed a change. The lights were all low and she saw the flicker of candlelight. Kendrick's arm tightened pulling her closer to his side, and he nuzzled behind her ear.

"A bath's been drawn for you. Why don't you go relax and cleanup while I check dinner? I'll join you in a few minutes."

She bit her lip, thinking of the huge tub in the center of Kendrick's enormous master bath, with the marble steps and greenery all around it. She'd wanted to sink into early, just to try it out. Feeling closer to him than ever, she wanted to experience *with* him, now.

"Hurry," she urged, holding his hand as she started to walk away and not letting go until their arms were stretched between them. She felt his absence the moment their fingers released. Almost the entire day, even in the helicopter touring the skyline, they'd continually touched. It was as if they had to be connected. They'd held hands, brushed fingers over the other's arm or leg, she'd lean her head on his shoulder, he'd kiss her somewhere... Just constant, inconsequential touches that had added up to a substantial connection wrapping around them and binding them together.

"I'll be there as soon as I check on things," he promised. "I expect you to be naked and in the tub when I get there." Though they'd just parted, he closed the space between them, grasped her hips and pulled her to him. His forehead leaned to hers. "No touching yourself while you wait," he rasped quietly.

"Or else?"

"Or else," he confirmed. "And it won't be a spanking for you to enjoy."

Moriah was half-tempted to push him and see what would happen if she defied him, but she wanted to prove she could obey him, too. She liked being naughty with him, but she wanted him to remember the good girl she'd been, too. She wanted to give Kendrick whatever pleasure she could, even if it was the pleasure of commanding her and her submitting to it.

Tipping her mouth closer to his, she brushed her lips across his. "Yes, sir," she whispered. "Naked and no touching. Got it."

144

He growled, and his fingers tightened on her waist. He turned her and gave her a gentle shove toward the bedroom. She giggled as she sprinted away, intent on following directions.

Sure they were alone and it was safe to undress, she started slipping off her dress on the way. She was down to her shoes when she entered the bedroom. She'd just kicked them off when she realized she wasn't alone.

An involuntary scream escaped. Panicked, she scrambled for the garment she'd just dropped.

"Moriah," Kendrick yelled. She heard him tearing down the hallway toward her as she stared at the unfamiliar dark-haired man, her dress clutched to her front. He made it to the door in long strides, closing and locking it before he closed it with a smirk on his face. A moment later, the knob rattled and Kendrick pounded.

She opened her mouth to yell, but the man shook his head and tapped his hand against his thigh, drawing her attention to the gun he held there.

"What do you want?" she asked in a strangled voice.

He scanned her barely covered body with hungry eyes and licked his bottom lip. "I've been sent to collect you."

"No." She wasn't sure he heard her over Kendrick's yelling and the bang of his fists on the wood. There was a loud thump of a body hitting the door. Oh God, Kendrick was going to force his way inside and this guy had a gun.

"Get your ass dressed before I shoot him through the door." He eyed the dress. "In something besides that thing you've been fucking him in."

"I—"

"Now."

"How did you get in here?" she asked, delaying.

"It doesn't fucking matter. Get your ass in gear or I won't be delivering you untouched—not that anyone would know if I had a taste for myself. It's not like you're a virgin anymore."

If her blood hadn't already gone cold, it would have been pure ice now. She edged toward the closet, keeping her front toward him, unwilling to show him her back or her naked backside.

"Who sent you to get me?" she asked as she reached blindly for a pile of clothes on the shelf just inside the closet door, hoping it was something she could wear. Thankfully, it was a pair of jeans and a T-shirt.

"Shut the fuck up and get dressed," he demanded, looking over his shoulder at the door. Apparently, realizing he wasn't coming through the well-constructed door, Kendrick had stopped banging himself against it. He wasn't yelling either.

Taking advantage of the man looking the other way, she yanked on the pants. She dropped the dress and tugged the tee quickly over her head, hating that she was once again without underwear. She hadn't cared that she wasn't fully covered while with Kendrick, but with this stranger, she wanted everything possible between the two of them.

"Shoes," he growled, picking up a pair of what were obviously women's runners.

"How do you plan to get out of here. He's not going to let you just waltz on out."

His hand shot out, closing around her neck. "I said to shut the fuck up!" He squeezed and her eyes watered. "You think he won't let me *waltz out of here* with a gun to your head?"

She made a choking sound and her eyes went wide. He smirked, thankfully not realizing her response was from the shadow moving in behind him, rather than him strangling her.

"Actually, it's the gun to your head, fucker," Kendrick snarled, his weapon jammed up to her would-be kidnappers temple. "Drop it and get your hand off her," he demanded. "Now, or this will be the last thing you know."

She stumbled backward as the intruder suddenly let her go. His gun thunked to the ground. Apparently, he realized Kendrick wasn't making idle thoughts. Her hand went to her throat as she gasped for air.

"Baby, are you okay?" he asked, keeping his full attention on the man.

"Yes," she rasped.

"Good. Head out to the living room to wait on the police, okay." He shoved the gun harder against his prisoner. "Put your hands on your head and follow her, asshole."

She stared at Kendrick, unable to move. Now that he was here, she shook like a leaf, on the edge of hyperventilating.

"It's okay, kitten. Go on."

"O-o-okay," she stammered. She edged around them and headed for the still-locked bedroom door. She glanced at him askance. How did he get in there?

"We'll talk about that later," he said, answering her unspoken question.

"Okay," she whispered and flipped the lock. Reality was slamming down heavily on her. Someone had just fucking tried to kidnap her. She'd been safe, feeling secure for once and someone had been...in Kendrick's sanctuary, ready to take here.

Moriah practically sprinted down the hallway, almost worried the man had an accomplice with him.

"Watch the security monitor in the front hall," Kendrick instructed. "They have the emergency code to get in, but you'll be able to see them coming."

"Okay." She seemed unable to get out any other words.

"Who sent you?" she heard Kendrick demand.

Silence greeted his question.

"How did you get in?"

149

The man chuckled. "Pretty easy with everyone you had running in and out of here for the little bitch."

She heard a thunk and a grunt. When she whipped her glance toward them she realized Kendrick had hit him with the gun. The intruder glared at her. "You're so not worth it," he growled.

"Want me to hit you again," Kendrick grated. "Say another word, and I'll knock you out until the cops deal with you."

The man snorted in response but held his tongue.

Moriah swung around when the elevator made a soft dinging sound to announce its arrival them the doors swooshed open. Several officers spilled out into the foyer, two heading directly toward Kendrick and his prisoner.

"We'll take it from here, Mr. Bergana," one of them said.

Kendrick immediately stepped away while they took command of the man. Kendrick set his weapon on a side table then grabbed Moriah to his chest. She sobbed leaning into him. The episode had been over before it had even really started, but she'd never been more terrified. And he'd saved her.

150

"Shh, it's okay, baby," he murmured. "I won't let anyone hurt you."

"But...but..."

"I promise. If I need to hire more security, I will. No one's hurting you."

"Sir," one of the officers interrupted. "We'd like to speak to you both about what happened."

Moriah looked up to see the bound intruder being led out of the penthouse. Her chest loosened slightly then she looked over at the blond cop who'd spoken.

"Certainly," Kendrick said. He indicated the living room. "Let's have a seat. I think Moriah needs to sit."

"Of course," the man said. "After you."

Kendrick led her into to one of the wide couches and seated her then wrapped a thick afghan around her shaking shoulders before he took his seat beside her and pulled her close to his side. She leaned her head to his shoulder, absorbing his strength and trying not to think about what would have happened if he hadn't gotten to her.

The cop pulled out his notebook. "The other officers are doing a sweep to be sure he didn't have a partner; is that all right, sir?"

"Of course," Kendrick replied without hesitation.

The man nodded. "I'm Detective Jenkins and this is my partner, Detective Jones." He nodded toward a man she hadn't realized had followed them. "Can you tell us what happened? You first, ma'am. Start with your name."

"It's Moriah Cabraro," she said, and his eyes widened slightly as if he recognized her name then immediately went impassive, and she thought maybe she'd imagined it. "I'm...I..."

"She's my fiancée," Kendrick inserted smoothly, rubbing his hand up and down her arm. She looked up him, her eyes wide with surprise. "We haven't announced it yet," he continued, giving her a tender smile. He indicated the candles around them and the warmers set up in the dining area on the patio just beyond the glass doors to outside. "We were getting ready to celebrate."

Moriah nodded, grateful for his subterfuge to protect her virtue and respectability. He could have told them she was staying her for the weekend, that they were just acquaintances, but instead, he'd made their relationship seem special.

"We just got back," she said, feeling stronger. "I was going to the bedroom to take a bath and change before we ate. That guy was in there waiting when I got there. I screamed, but he locked the door before I could get out or Kendrick could get to me."

"Do you know who he is?"

She shook her head. "He said he'd come to collect me, whatever that means. He threatened to shoot Kendrick through the door if I didn't cooperate. He threated to...rape me...if I didn't do as he said."

Kendrick's arm tightened. "Jesus," he muttered, and she felt the shudder that went through him. Not fear. Rage. Glancing at his face, she suspected he'd murder that guy if he were still here.

"I don't know how he planned to get out of there, but he made me put on something other than the dress I had on. He started to choke me when I asked questions." She lifted her chin to show her neck that still throbbed, unsure whether there were marks or not.

Kendrick kissed the top of her head and took a deep inhalation, seeming to breathe her in to calm himself.

"When I realized what was happening, I tried to get through the door, but I couldn't," Kendrick explained, sounding mighty pissed off that his sturdy door had flummoxed him. "I called 9-1-1, then I went to the bedroom beside mine. The balcony adjoins. This high up, I don't always lock the door, and even if it was, I could have broken through. I was able to get in, grab the gun from my bedside table and come up beside him before he knew I was there."

"Thank God," she whispered.

"You said he claimed he was here to collect you. Do you have any idea who sent him?"

She shook her head. "No, not really."

Maybe one of the men who hadn't won the auction, but she didn't want to tell them that or admit having any part of the tawdry affair.

"Possibly her father," Kendrick offered. "He's been embezzling from my company and is trying to use Moriah as a pawn to get me to forgive him."

"You've reported this?"

"No." He shook his head. "We were keeping it inhouse. I gave him until Monday to repay me. Failing that, all the documentation would be released to the board and charges filed. I didn't want to wait, so we had a preemptive meeting scheduled for tomorrow afternoon with someone from your department to discuss the situation. I'm sorry, I don't have the specific information from my assistant off the top of my head, but I can get that for you in a few moments."

"Please," Jenkins said, and Kendrick pulled out his phone.

"Would your father send someone to take you against your will?" Jones asked.

"I don't put anything past him anymore. I never thought he'd steal millions from my…fiancé."

Kendrick half-laughed beside her. He looked at the officer across from her. "Apparently, I'm supposed to meet with you and Detective Jones. He scheduled it as a representative from *Berg Trade*."

The man nodded, apparently recognizing the appointment. "Seems we have a lot more than embezzling to discuss then. Our white-collar crime division is doing most of the investigation.

The documentation and files they reviewed were cut and dry, like he didn't even bother to cover his tracks. But now it seems we might have more to deal with now. There's a child involved?"

"My younger sister, Jade Cabraro."

They discussed Jade's living conditions and Jofre's threats. Moriah told them about Jofre threatening her to get her to do what he wanted, that he'd wanted her to sell herself for the money but stopped short of telling them what she'd actually done.

"You should know Mr. Cabraro was already under investigation—"

"For what?" Moriah asked before she could stop herself.

"Alleged trafficking."

"What?" she exclaimed, though she supposed she shouldn't be surprised. She shuddered as she realized her plight could have been so much worse—and if he'd sent that man to take her, she could have been on the brink of something from which she never would have survived.

He closed his notebook and frowned when at the look his partner gave him. Jenkins turned back to Jones. "I'm going to hear all about that I shouldn't have told you that."

"No, you shouldn't have," Jones, the older of the two men, injected with clear censure.

Moriah held up her hands. "I didn't hear anything. I just want my sister safely away from him." Even if Jade became a temporary ward of the state, Moriah had to believe she'd be safer than with her father.

Kendrick pulled her against his chest as they stood to see the officers out. "And I just want you safe," he said against her hair. She sagged against him as soon as they were alone.

"The bath is probably cold by now," he said.

"I just want to go to sleep," she murmured. It wasn't that late, but she was exhausted.

"You should eat."

"I can't."

He nodded. "All right. Why don't you go climb into bed, and I'll clean up—"

"I don't want to be alone." It was probably foolish; the cops had checked the entire place. She just didn't feel safe by herself.

"Okay, baby," he replied, seeming to understand. "Stay here on the couch. You'll be able to see me while I take care of things."

Drawing the blanket tighter around herself, she sat again. She didn't realize she'd fallen asleep until she felt Kendrick carrying her. She was vaguely aware of him disrobing her, tucking her beneath the blankets then sitting beside her as he quietly spoke on the phone. Then he was next to her, holding her tight in his arms as if he were afraid she'd sneak away — or someone would take her.

Chapter Fourteen

Kendrick sat up in bed, clutching his bare chest, sensing something was off. Moriah wasn't next to him like she should be. Panic wrenched his lungs, especially when he saw it was four in the morning.

"Illuminate," he commanded the lights in his bedroom.

The pants he'd pulled off Moriah when he'd put her to bed still remained crumpled on the floor where he'd dropped them. He scrambled off the mattress and, while dragging on a pair of sweatpants, rushed into the bathroom— she wasn't there. If someone had taken her, surly he would have woken, but reasoning with himself did little to quell his thudding heart.

He left his room, sought out the light in his office, and found Moriah sitting at his desk, in a T-shirt and panties. It took all his willpower not to pull her up, bend her over and spank the new underwear off her little rear end for the scare she'd given him. She was supposed to be in bed, not trying to break into his computer.

"Moriah," he said as he drew near. "What are you doing?"

"I have to know," she sobbed. "I have to find out."

His lingering panic and frustration melted away to anxiety. He knelt beside her and carefully spun her chair to face him. "Know what? Talk to me, Moriah. Why are you crying?"

"All the women. All the young women my father used to bring home, even while my mother was dying from cancer. They never stayed around long—I saw them once or twice, and now, I worry…" She smothered her distress with a palm over her mouth.

"Oh, kitten," he murmured softly, pulling her from the chair and into his arms. She joined him on the floor, holding him so tight as if to never let go.

"I just assumed they were… I don't know," she hiccupped. "They were probably trafficked, sold off to whoever by my father, and I didn't do anything to stop it."

He smoothed her hair off her tear-stained face. "You can't think that way. We don't know if the allegations are true," he said, taking the 'innocent until proven guilty' stance. "Do you have any contact with these women? Are they missing?"

"No, I didn't want to keep in touch with them," she lamented. "I didn't bother to get to know them or even ask them their names. I was too resentful. I thought they were gold diggers looking for a sugar daddy, but now…"

He placed his finger over her lips. "Then what did you hope to find on the computer?"

"I don't know—something. Anything."

"Okay. Listen. This isn't your guilt to bear, kitten. You couldn't have known what your father was doing with these women, if he even did anything wrong. He might be innocent of the trafficking allegations."

Moriah pulled backward from his finger and gave him a skeptical frown. "Please, Kendrick. He sold my virginity to the highest bidder in some awful auction he managed to setup in under three days. How did he even know people like that—people who'd buy things

161

like *that*—if he hadn't done something like *that* before?"

Kendrick didn't want to agree, if only to spare her the likely truth, so he deflected. "Let's go to bed. You can call the detectives tomorrow."

"Some of the women weren't even from around here. He met them on oversea on business trips. Oh my God," she cried, as if realizing the implications.

"Then we can call the FBI if that will help," he assured, "but I believe Detectives Jenkins and Jones are already in touch with a taskforce. The point is, there's nothing *you* could have done differently. You were a child and hindsight is always 20-20. Traffickers are master manipulators and, unfortunately, are often too good at what they do. They know how to hide their crimes and avoid detection, even from family and friends."

"You're right," she conceded. "I… With that asshole wanting to 'collect' me… I might have been one of those women if you hadn't bought me, and now, I'm targeted."

Kendrick captured her face in his palms. "No. No one will take you from me. No one. You got that?"

She nodded, dislodging more tears.

"Let me hear you say it," he demanded.

"No one will take me away from you. I am safe with you," she whispered.

"I mean it, Moriah. You're mine. I love you. I protect what is mine."

Moriah suddenly kissed him, long and hard and deep and desperate. Then she pulled away and ripped her T-shirt off, tossing it behind her before ravaging his lips again. Her aggressive seduction was a blatant a sign, and he recognized her need to control *something — anything —* in her life, especially now.

He allowed her to proceed as she wanted, passively returning her attentions without taking the lead.

Moriah delved her hands downward and into his sweatpants. She gripped his already hard dick and stroked it a couple times before she pulled it from the fabric constraints. Kendrick moved her panties to the side as she guided the head toward her entrance.

She let all her weight drop on his cock, her pussy gliding down his girth with snug ease. He groaned as her heat enveloped him. The tight vise of her walls tested his determination to let her take the lead. It was heaven and hell; pleasure and pure torture. He wouldn't change a thing.

Moriah rode him hard and fast, grunting and panting and crying and moaning, as if trying to fuck away all the bad feelings plaguing her. Kendrick did what he could without impeding her, which had him supporting her hips while her breasts bounced in his face. He leaned forward and capture one between his lips, sucking it deep while he yelled out her approval, her arms circling his head and holding him there. Not a problem. He'd give her whatever she needed. With each draw of his mouth, he felt the corresponding clench of her pussy around him, milking his cock to the end of his endurance. He wasn't sure how much longer he could hold out.

Thankfully, her climax was strong and quick to arrive, with her screaming and digging her fingernails into his shoulders as she ground her pussy down on him.

"Fuck," he growled, thrusting impossibly deeper. He kept plunging into her as she cried out, pleasure and possibly some pain propelling her into a second, stronger orgasm.

As she rode the waves of ecstasy, Kendrick withdrew then drove into her again, and again, and again, until she shrieked like a demon possessed. The pulsing clasp of her walls pulled him over the edge. An explosion of pleasure went through him, and his cum spilled into her tight grip. Beyond reason, he wished his seed could take hold and bind her to her even more than the tenuous feelings between them.

After long moments, they both returned to themselves. With damp foreheads pressed together, they breathed each other's air as they panted. When they finally caught their breaths, he murmured, "I love you."

"I love you," she whispered.

Kendrick's world rocked. It was her first time saying that to him. Obviously, he'd known she felt deeply for him—her eyes said what her lips didn't—but to hear the words moved him more than he cared to admit.

"We should go back to bed. Let's go back to bed," he said.

* * * *

Kendrick had stayed awake to watch Moriah sleep. When seven AM rolled around, he rose from the bed and ran a bath for her. She'd asked to go to church, so to church she would go. He figured it would be good for her. She'd find comfort there. After all, her spirituality was important to her, and therefore, it was now important to him, too. He would see her there then back home safely.

When the bathtub was filled with hot, bubbly water and the fireplace was roaring, he went to collect Moriah from the bed.

"Rise and shine, kitten,"

She moaned and batted at him to leave her alone then rolled over to give him her back. He wasn't having that. He simply lifted her from the bed and carried her toward the bathroom. She groaned her displeasure at being disturbed.

"I'd hate to have to wake you up with a spanking."

That got her attention. Her eyes flew open as he put her on her feet. She stared him down. "Why? Because you woke me up? Maybe, I should give you a spanking."

He chuckled. "You wanted to go to church. And your bath is ready."

Moriah spun around, and her irritation melted into delight. "Oh, wow! Thank you so much." Since she only wore panties, she was naked and in the tub in no time. He picked up the underwear and deposited it into the hamper. He figured he should retrieve her pants from his bedroom floor and her shirt from his office.

"This feels so good," she cooed. "You should join me."

166

"We won't make it to church if I join you."

She had the audacity to smirk. "Can't control yourself, huh?"

Kendrick lifted his brow then promptly dropped his sweats. "Fine. I'll join you. But if our bath escalates into something more than bathing, I'll paddle your ass—with a paddle. Got it?"

Moriah huffed and folded her arms. "Please. I can control myself."

So he joined her in the large tub, sitting opposite of her. There was a lot of room. Kendrick couldn't remember the last time he'd had a bath. He was more of a shower man. But as long as Moriah wanted him with her, he could change over.

They sat in silence and stared at each other. It was almost as if they were daring each other to do something—or perhaps, she was afraid to do more for fear of that spanking he'd threatened earlier. He loved the firelight reflecting off her body and the way the water droplets rolled over her smooth skin. He enjoyed the glimpses of her breasts as the bubbles parted with her small movements.

He enjoyed the peeks too much. His dick was hard yet again.

"Let me wash you," she said.

"I should be washing you."

Moriah shook her head. "You always take care of me. Let me take care of you."

"Hmm." But he allowed her to float over to him, where she settled between his legs. She smiled, obviously feeling the erection pressing into her while she reached over his shoulder to collect the soap and sponge. She leaned back and straddled him, her breasts firm and high and on display for his perusal. She rubbed her palms together until a scented froth formed and dropped from her fingertips. His cock ached at being so close to her heat yet so far away.

The soap, released from her grip, splashed into the water. She placed the lathered sponge on his chest and lazily circled around, her free hand following the foamy path left behind by her ministrations as if to massage the suds into his skin.

Then she leaned forward and wrapped her arms around his neck, her nipples swaying in his face like ripe cherries ready for picking on a breezy day, and proceeded to wash his shoulders and back. He swallowed a groan and resisted the urge to suck a taut bud between his lips, even as his mouth watered with the possibility of tasting her sweetness.

It wouldn't do for him to lose his self-control. Not only would she get to spank him, but they were supposed to go to church soon.

"Okay," he said, pulling the sponge from her fingers. "Let's get washed up." And with a focused hand, he proceeded to wash her quickly. She giggled at the rough, practical scrubbing. He didn't know if she were simply ticklish or laughing at his obvious discomfort. His dick was so hard it was painful. Fuck. He hadn't had blue balls since he was a teen.

"Out you go," he announced.

"My hair?" she said with a vixen's grin.

"We'll revisit this after church. I washed the parts that matter, so that you could go to the altar without shame, considering what we did earlier this morning," he said.

She huffed at him in mock offense, but she rose up. "I guess I should go to confession for my shameful behavior this weekend."

On his feet, he kissed her hard. "I was kidding. Nothing we do is shameful. If anything, it's quite the opposite. It's beautiful. Making love with you is heaven on earth as far as I'm concerned."

"Aw," she said, a blush tingeing her cheeks beyond the pink there from the steam and heat. "Maybe, we should skip church."

Kendrick smacked her ass and helped her from the tub. "Go put on a pretty dress, kitten. We're going to Mass."

Chapter Fifteen

Sunday had passed in a blur. Going to church, as simple as that might seem, had been amazing with Kendrick at her side, and once it was over, she felt as if she really could make it through the next weeks and she wasn't alone.

Afterward, her fed her—successfully. She'd had to tease him about that. All weekend, it had seemed as if he'd plan to feed her then something would get in the way or sidetrack them or cut the meal short. They'd actually spent over an hour at the table until "the way you're fucking sipping that coffee" had made him wild and he'd spread her out right there on the table and fucked her like a madman, in a very unholy way.

Just thinking that had given her the giggles, and when she'd confessed why she couldn't stop laughing, he'd thrown her over his shoulder and taken her to the bedroom to show her more of his naughty inclinations, though he'd reminded her that whatever they did was okay between the two of them because they loved each other.

And she did love him. She believed that she'd still be with him after this weekend was over. Truly, it was hard for her to fathom, but that didn't stop her from the merit she put to his words. He seemed completely okay with Jade being part of their life. too. Good thing. It wouldn't have mattered how much she loved him, if he didn't want Jade to be part of their future, it would have been a deal breaker. His only caveat was that he wanted children of his own, too.

That had come a few minutes ago. Moriah looked over at him in the fading afternoon light. It was early evening, but this portion of his penthouse faced east and darkened sooner than on the west side. She rolled into him, feeling replete after long hours of making love and discovering all the sensual pleasures between them—well, maybe not all, she acknowledged, but more than she'd imagined. It wasn't all about fucking. In fact, little of their time in this bed had involved penetration with his cock. Fingers…tongue…there'd been a lot of that.

She rested her head on his shoulder and trailed her fingers along his chest, between his pecs and down to his flat belly then back up. Back and forth, lulling them both.

"You want kids with me?" she asked.

"Oh yeah," he breathed. The arm around her tightened and he kissed her forehead.

"How many?"

He shrugged. "As many as you want to give me, but I hope at least three or four."

"That's a lot."

"You think so?"

"Well...with Jade, we'll be wrangling five children."

"Hmm," he replied, the sound full of pleasure and zero question.

She poked his ribs. "And you don't have to have them. I would."

"I'd be there every second of the way."

She smiled, completely sure he would be. Over the years, she'd seen how he operated. He invested himself in his pet interests. The way he talked, she thought perhaps she'd joined that group.

"Do you not want any children?" he asked. "I'd never force you…"

"No, I do."

"Good." He sighed. "We need to get up soon. Your detective pals are coming over in an hour."

She groaned at the reminder of the upheaval in her life and all of the allegations against her father, many of which she knew were true because of her personal involvement, if one could call her victimization that. She and Kendrick couldn't possibly start planning for their future when so much still laid in the balance. Moriah wasn't sure she'd ever be free of her father's reach, prison or not. She and Jade might need to go into hiding. Hell, he might get off scot-free then destroy her. A cold rail of fear spiked through her at the idea.

Needing to do something to escape her thoughts, she slipped from the bed and headed toward the bathroom. She heard him sit up behind her, but she shut the door between them, hoping he realized she needed a few minutes alone.

There was a light tap on the door as she gripped the edge of the counter and stared at herself in the mirror. "Kitten, are you okay?"

"Yeah, I'm good," she replied quickly, maybe too quickly because the doorknob turned and he came in.

"Geez, Kendrick. I just needed a second," she groused. He didn't say a word, just crossed the space and pulled her into his arms. This hand went to the back of her head and pressed her to his chest.

"It's going to be all right," he promised, rocking her slightly. "I know there's so much going on, so much more heavy shit than I ever imagined, but I will protect you and see you through this."

"I don't know if you can."

"I can. I'll do everything in my power to ensure your safety."

"But...what if it's beyond your power?" she whispered.

"Love, there's very little outside my power."

She huffed a watery laugh. "You're a little full of yourself."

175

"No, I'm just fully aware of the sway of cash, lots of cash. I've got plenty of options, inside and outside the law, if it comes to that."

"I don't want you to do anything that will get you in trouble."

"Too late for that."

"What?" she gasped. What had he done?

He pulled back and looked her in the eye. "Going to that auction, *buying you* from that auction, wasn't exactly aboveboard."

"But you saved me," she protested. Oh God, she didn't want him to get in trouble for helping her.

"That's the only saving grace, trust me. I have plenty of people I can pull in to spin that fact into me being a damn superhero."

"My superhero."

"Yours."

"Does that mean you'll wear a cape?" She could imagine the sexy games they could play...

He shook his head. "Too dangerous," he replied with faux-seriousness, and she marveled at how he could pull her out of despair so easily. He understood her and knew what she needed.

"But…" she bit her lip. "I could be the damsel in distress and you could come in in nothing but your big cape—"

"No."

"It could be sexy and fun. Oh! I could be the inept villainess and you could swoop in wearing nothing but that cape and put me over your—"

"Do you have some sort of comic book hero fetish we should discuss?"

"I never thought so, but…" She reached between them and stroked his hard, long length. "I'm betting you're quite the man of steel."

"The only man of steel you'll ever know."

She hoped that was true. Well, she doubted she'd ever want anyone else. *Ever.*

Moriah smiled up at him. "Thank you."

His brow furrowed. "For…what?"

"Making me feel better when I get to far into my head. Making me feel safe. Buying me.

Bringing me here. Loving me." She shrugged and looked away.

His fingers lightly grasped her chin, bringing her gaze back to his. "I do love you. And you never need to thank me for those things." He brushed his lips over hers, and she shivered at the warm prickles of belonging that cascaded over her. Before the kiss could go further, he pulled back. "We really need to get ready, so we're not naked and smelling like sex when the detectives get here. Not that I mind if you do. I want to warn off any assholes who get too close."

"*I* mind!" she protested.

"Should I be offended by that?"

She rolled her eyes. "You know how you don't want anyone hearing me come? Well, I don't want to share our sex with anyone else, either."

He chuckled and kissed the center of her forehead before moving away to start the shower.

* * * *

Dressed in a sleeveless, sapphire-blue dress, Moriah sat on the wide couch beside Kendrick and looked back and forth between Jenkins and Jones who sat in armchairs facing them. She fingered the ring he'd slipped onto her left hand before they'd gotten there. It was so beautiful, a large princess-cut pink diamond surrounded smaller white diamonds. She wished she'd get to keep it, that is was her real engagement ring, but she had no idea where he'd gotten it or why he had it.

"So let me get this straight," Jenkins said as he consulted his notebook.

Moriah's cheeks burned. She hated this. She felt so violated just having to talk about it.

"Last Friday, Mr. Bergana purchased you from an auction your father set up for the sole purpose of procuring the money to pay back the money he'd embezzled from Mr. Bergana's company."

"Yes, but Kendrick could never let that happen. He had to step in before anything happened to me."

Both detectives looked slightly skeptical. "Okay," Jones said. "And you didn't call the police why?"

"Because—"

The detective cut off Kendrick. "Only Ms. Cabraro."

179

"Um…" she cleared her throat. "If I betrayed him, if I didn't go along with his plan, he threatened to take out his anger at me on my little sister. I didn't feel like I had a choice. And no offense but we thought the police couldn't act fast enough, especially with it taking place out of the country. I'm not even sure what country has jurisdiction over that island."

"We can find out. Do you know the location of the island?"

She shook her head. "My father arranged all the travel."

"He provided coordinates but no further details on the mansion. My pilot had to file a flight plan. It was to an island off the Brazilian coast," Kendrick offered.

"I don't think it was the first time he's done this," Moriah blurted out. Those women had been on her mind most of the time today — when Kendrick hadn't distracted her. She went on to explain her suspicions to them. She gasped as another sickening thought occurred to her. "We've had maids just suddenly quit, just never show up again." She turned to Kendrick. "Oh my God do you think…?"

"I don't know, love." He pulled her closer to his side and leaned his head into her.

"Does he keep files at your home? Perhaps files that are always locked?" Jones inquired.

Moriah nodded. "No one's allowed into his office unless he orders them come see him. He doesn't even let the staff clean in there."

"Do you have enough to get a warrant to search?" Kendrick asked.

"It's thin," Jenkins admitted.

"Even with my story and whatever else you've been investigating?" she asked.

"We do have probable cause, and with Ms. Cabraro's information, we have a good chance of having the warrant issued. We'll get the affidavit before the judge this evening. Since we doubt Mr. Cabraro is an overnight flight risk at this point, since he's expecting you home in the morning, that's when we'll be expected to execute the warrant."

"What about the attempted kidnapping?" she asked. "Am I going to need to look over my shoulder constantly after this?"

"No. The people surrounding your father work for cash—as in, they expect to be paid. From what we've been able to learn, the man who broke in was hired off the street. He was wanted for several B&Es but he's not professional when it

181

comes to kidnapping. As soon as Mr. Cabraro's accounts are frozen, he won't have access to hire another to come after you."

"Baby, as my fiancée then as my wife, you'll have security on you at all times. I'm too high-profile for you not to."

"Okay," she said to the room at large. She wasn't sure how she felt about having her own detail but the weight on her did inexplicably lighten a little at the thought.

Jenkins slid away his notebook then level an assessing look at her. "This is touchy," he started. "But is your father armed, does he have a gun in the house?"

"He has a gun, but he doesn't carry it."

"Would you be willing to wear a wire to go in and speak to him tomorrow? To discuss what he did to you? And the disappearance of the other women you've thought of? Or even to ask about their names?"

"No," Kendrick answered for her.

She looked over at him in surprise and shook her head. "I have to."

"No, you don't," he exclaimed in disbelief. "No way."

"You'll be there? You'd keep me safe?" she asked the two detectives.

"Of course. Out of sight, but there."

She nodded. "I'll do it."

Kendrick shot to his feet, shoving his hands into his hair as he paced away. Moriah got the feeling they were going to have a fight once the officers departed, and not like the mild disagreements they'd had so far. Tension and anger vibrated off him to a degree she'd never seen. She knew he wouldn't hurt her, but it frightened her nonetheless.

"Mr. Bergana—"

"This is bullshit!" he exploded. "You're asking my fiancée, the woman I love, to go into that monster's home and put herself in danger."

"I owe it to all those women I hated when I should have been helping them," she pleaded.

"You were a *child!*"

"And now I'm not and I can make my own decisions. Maybe, I can help them."

From the faces around her, she knew that was slim.

"Or give closure," she whispered. "And keep it from happening again," she added in a much stronger voice.

"Don't try to make me agree to this."

"You don't have to. It's my decision."

When Kendrick turned to fully face her at her, the tension in his jaw had turned his skin white over the bones. A muscled ticked frantically in his cheek. His chest rose and fell harshly as he panted, and if she didn't know better, she'd have believed he was about to hulk out.

Moriah crossed to him and placed her hand on his arm. "Please try to understand."

"That you want to do something absolutely foolish that will put you in danger? No. No, I won't try to understand that."

"Kendrick—"

He walked away from her and left her alone with the officers. She looked over at them helplessly, embarrassed by the scene. They were looking around the living room, out the window, at the ceiling, clearly trying to not be there even though they were in the space with Moriah and Kendrick. She jumped when she heard a door slam. Kendrick's office, she supposed.

"I'm sorry," she ventured.

"It's all right, ma'am. I have to say, I understand his position. If it was my wife, I'd feel the same way. If you don't want to do this..." Jones said.

"I don't *want* to. I need to."

"All right."

"And Jade?"

"Mr. Bergana has been in touch with someone, because the paperwork already came through, stating she is to go with you."

"Senator McKenzie," she offered, not that it mattered who had pushed this through. Kendrick had done this for her, too. She just wished he could understand her need to do what she could. It was a relief to know Jade would be safe in her care after tomorrow, however.

She glanced toward the hallway, concerned about Kendrick.

"Look..." Jones ventured. "With your information, along with Mr. Bergana's corroborating story, we already have enough to arrest Mr. Cabraro. Once he's arrested, we can conduct our search. You don't need to go in with the wire. We're already working with the FBI and

Department of Homeland Security on this. They're going to want to speak with you and obtain any information you have, as well as anything else Mr. Bergana can offer, such as the names of those involved."

"I don't know them."

"I do," Kendrick said, reentering the living room. He handed over a folder to Detective Jenkins who was closest to him. "This is all the information I have on the auction, including the coordinates, who did the medical evaluations and those people I recognized in attendance."

"Holy shit," Jenkins muttered under his breath as he flipped through the file. Moriah's cheeks flamed at what she knew he was seeing in there. Personal things she wished no one else would ever see. No one but Kendrick ever needed to know this that stuff and even then, some of it she'd rather have kept to herself.

"I've included contact information for my pilot. I've spoken with him and given him permission to talk with you. He'll tell you whatever you need to know about the trip." He turned to Moriah. "I don't want you putting yourself in danger."

"Mr. Bergana, I must ask you, had you ever attended something like this before that night?"

"God, no," he spat in disgust. "I was only there for Moriah. Do I need to contact my attorney?"

"Frankly, for a man in your position, I'm surprised you haven't already, but no. You aren't under investigation."

"If you don't mind, I'll bring the head of my legal team into the know. I haven't done anything wrong, except for attending the auction to save Moriah, but I'd rather he be prepared if the tide turns."

Jones nodded. "His name, please."

Kendrick provided the name.

"I should be there for Jade," she said, looking over at Kendrick and wondering if she was going to piss him off again but knowing her sister would need her.

"But out of the way," he said.

"Okay," she replied in relief.

They wrapped up with the detectives, and after they'd seen the men out, Kendrick pulled

187

her into his arms. "I can't let anything happen to you," he whispered into her hair. "I know it might seem fast, but losing you… I wouldn't recover."

She pressed into his chest. "I can't lose you either," she whispered. She looked up at him. "Kendrick?"

"Yes, kitten?"

"Take me to bed."

With a single, solemn nod, he lifted her into his arm and she wrapped her arms around his neck. He was her safety. And she was his.

Chapter Sixteen

Kendrick laid her on the bed then stepped back to take off his clothes. Moriah scrambled up and dropped to her knees before him. He groaned when she reached for his pants. She took that as encouragement and quickly popped open the button and pulled down the zip. Unable to help herself, she nuzzled his cock where it bulged behind his black boxer-briefs. Her mouth watered as she remembered the first night when she'd taken him in her mouth. And yesterday in the garden. Considering she'd never given head before, she was quickly coming to love his reaction to her mouth on him.

Wanting more of the same, she pulled down his underwear and shoved them down his legs with his pants. Kendrick stood absolutely still, not even kicking off his shoes or the clothes along his legs. Just waiting.

She looked up at him and found his gaze burning down at her, his eyes dark with lust. "Put your mouth on me," he commanded. "Do it now."

She swallowed, the order causing her pussy to clench with need.

"Mouth only," he snapped out when she reached for him. Her eyes widened while other parts of her went hot and wet. She swallowed then parted her lips and leaned into him. Moriah hummed as his glans slide against her tongue and she tasted his creamy pre-cum. Her fingers clenched at her sides, as she reminded herself not to take him in hand.

After barely a moment, Kendrick pulled free. The tip of his length dragged wetly across her chin. "Who do you belong to?" he demanded.

"Y-you."

"Then why did you insist on defying me? And in front of other people?"

"I—"

"There is no excuse, Moriah. You're mine to protect. You're mine, period. You promised to obey me."

"But…that was…"

190

"Before you knew this was real? Forever? Before you realized you're completely mine? Did you think the rules changed?"

"No, but we weren't in the bedroom. That was real life, not our sex life."

"Fine," he ground out. "Then we need a renegotiation."

"Now?" She didn't like the sound of that. Not right now when she was on her knees and so needy for him.

"You will obey me in the bedroom—in any sexual situation—just as we previously agreed."

"All right," she conceded, nodding to underline her agreement.

"And in any situation that might put you in danger."

That seemed really vague. Her face scrunched as she squinted at him. "Define what you mean by that."

"Something that could injure you enough to see a doctor or that might endanger your life."

"Like...driving."

He raised an eyebrow at her. "You don't drive. In the future, your security detail will or I will drive you wherever you want to go."

"And if I want to drive? I know how, by the way. I have a license." This was ridiculous. They were debating driving with her on her knees, his naked cock less than a foot from her mouth. She moved to get up.

"Stay there," he commanded.

She sighed and rolled her eyes.

"This isn't about driving, and you know it," he went on. "But since it seems to be an issue for you—" It wasn't really her problem. All indications pointed to it being his hang-up. "—can we compromise on the driving being outside the city?"

She shrugged. "Okay."

"And the rest?"

"Yes, I agree to obey you in the bedroom."

"And?"

"And I won't rush into danger. And I'll let you protect me. And I'll listen to your concerns. And I'll take my punishment when I think you're full of shit and exercise my freewill anyway."

"Moriah…" he warned.

"Mostly the first part, okay? I promise I'll listen to you. I love you, and I don't want you worrying about me all the time. And if I *accidentally* endanger myself, you can spank me…or whatever."

"Better."

"But you have to remember I have a mind of my own, and despite indications otherwise, I really have been taking care of myself for a really long time."

"I know." He smiled sadly and let out a long breath. "But you don't have to anymore. And just in case you don't know, I happen to be rather enamored with that naughty, willful, inventive mind of yours."

She grinned, having managed to negotiate that minefield. It warmed her to hear him praise her, and she hoped they were on the same page, and not just in the same book. While some feminists might protest she'd given too much away, she wouldn't complain at all about the power equation between her and Kendrick. She had a guy who wanted nothing more than to keep her safe. He wasn't taking away her rights; he was just asking her to listen to him and let him protect her. She wasn't big on danger anyway. Risks made her queasy.

"I love you, too," he added.

"I know. Can I..." She smirked, rethinking her wording then pulled a solemn, puppy-dog-eyed look, batting her eyelashes slightly. "Would it please sir for me to suck his cock now?"

"You are such a brat."

She stayed silent. For him, she was kind of bratty.

"Yes, get to it," he replied.

Happily, she leaned forward and wrapped her lips around him again, focusing on the crown of his long length. Kendrick groaned as she pressed the tip of her tongue against it, seeking more of his pre-cum.

"Are you sure this is new to you?" he asked as she took more of him into her mouth. "Your skills are good for a recently former virgin. You better not have been practicing on—"

She pulled back quickly, shaking her head. "Only you!" she promised.

"Good," he growled, his hand burying in her hair and pulling her back to the task. "Only ever me."

Moriah liked the sound of that, and her body reacted to his possessive words, clenching and moistening for his eventual penetration. She moaned around his length then sucked hard while pulling back.

"Oh fuck," he grunted. His fingers tightened in her hair and she let up a little, but only so she could take him to her throat. She gagged a little, her eyes watering.

"You're doing so good, feels so good," he muttered. "Such a good kitten."

His words encouraged her, and she kept going, getting more and more turned on as he got closer to release, his sounds growing guttural, his breathing choppy.

"Fuck, Moriah. Fuck. Fuck. Your little mouth... Fuck baby."

She would have smiled at his unspoken praise but it only made her more in tent on making him come.

"Oh...*fuck*. No!" he suddenly exclaimed, wrenching free. A moment later, Kendrick had her bent over the bed, her skirt up and her panties ripped off. He kicked her stance wider. Then his cock surged into her and he fucked her hard. Moriah clawed at the blankets, screaming into them as he drove in and out in a fury. So perfect. So wild.

"Kendrick," she yelled. "God, yes. Harder," she encouraged though she didn't know if that was possible. He seemed possessed, his fingers digging into her hips, holding her still for his deep thrusts.

"Mine," he grated out. "Mine. No one hurts you. No one touches you. No one takes you from me."

His tension and anger had only been temporarily hidden. Obviously, the idea of her going into danger made him snap, and now, all she could do was hold on for the storm.

"No…I promise," she cried. What she was promising? Could she really say she'd always be safe? Not to put herself in danger on purpose. In the storm that was Kendrick right this moment, he was the most dangerous thing to her wellbeing, yet she knew he'd never hurt her.

Closing her eyes and grappling for a hold on the bed, she let her body take over and fully unite with him, two pieces of a whole slamming together as a perfect fit. The exquisite friction along her walls, of his base slamming against her clit with each deep drive, of his body over hers, owning, claiming… It all drove her to a place of sensation without thought or problems or the future. They were just now. In this moment. One.

"Kendrick!" she yelled as her pussy clamped around him and her vision grayed. Then she couldn't breathe, her muscles locking into a frozen arch beneath him.

"Oh fuck, yeah. You're so wet and tight around me." He gasped out harsh, uneven breaths as he kept thrusting. "You're like a fucking vise, taking everything. You want everything from me, don't you? You want it?"

"I want it," she cried. "Please." Moriah needed him to fill her, craved his warmth exploding into her, marking her as his again.

"Nothing is like being inside you. Can't…ever…be without…it," he managed and then with one final hard drive, his guttural yell joined her as he came, his climax tumbling her off into another blast of indescribable bliss.

She was a limp, innervated mess when she became somewhat aware of their surroundings again. A haze of utter wellbeing blanketed her, so warm and mussy, like she floated on a wave of nothingness, without a worry in the world.

Kendrick had pushed aside her hair and was kissing her neck. When he trailed down her spine, she realized he'd unzipped her dress

"I love you," she mumbled, smiling into the blankets, her eyes closed.

He chuckled and pressed a firm kiss between her shoulder blades. "Are you going to sleep on me?"

"Mm-hmm. Maybe. Don't wanna… When I wake up it will be Monday."

He rolled her over then waited to speak until she opened her eyes to look up at him. He smiled tenderly at her. "And that's okay, because Monday is the start of our life together without your father and his threats hanging over our heads, without the worry of him trying to rip us apart, without you having to worry about what he might do to your sister. Tomorrow will be a good day, kitten. And tomorrow, like today and every day afterward, you will be mine. And I will love you and cherish you and make sure you have anything you ever desire."

"I just want you with me and for Jade to be safe. I don't need anything else."

"Done. Now…" He nuzzled against her throat. "Are you awake again? I have this desperate need to make love to you all night."

She hummed, closing her eyes and stretching like a cat beneath him — or like a kitten, as he called her. "I think I like that plan."

Chapter Seventeen

Moriah rolled into Kendrick and smacked her face into his hip. She groaned then fell over onto her back and opened her eyes.

"Why aren't you asleep?" she mumbled, staring up at him where he say beside her, his back propped against the headboard, his tablet in his hand.

"Morning, sweetheart," he chuckled. Why was he up and working and so damn cheerful? He'd kept her most of the night—not that she was complaining about that. But how could he look so wide awake? "I'm just working on a few things before we start our day. You should go back to sleep. No need to get moving for a couple hours yet."

He smiled tenderly down at her, his fingers stroking through her hair. The slow, repetitive movement, along with the security and warmth of having him right there lulled her back to sleep. So it was a shock when she popped awake in the sun-flooded room totally alone. A glance at the clock showed it was after eight.

She sat up, looking around. Kendrick wasn't in the room and through the open bathroom door, she could see he wasn't in there either. Total silence weighed heavy throughout his home, broken only by the distant hum and occasional honk from the traffic on the street well below her.

After climbing from bed, she padded down the hall toward his office, thinking he'd decided to get in some work there while she slept. Empty. Brow furrowed she headed toward the kitchen. Empty. The open floorplan revealed he was nowhere in the common space. For good measure, she peeked out onto the patio surrounding the pool. Empty.

Moriah didn't bother checking the other rooms. Instinctively, she knew. A leaden weight settled in her gut as she realized he was gone. It was Monday morning. It was over. The weekend was over. Why had he said all those things to make her believe he wanted more than the past couple days? It was like some sick joke!

Breathing deeply, focusing on pushing air in and out through her nose, she covered her mouth with her hand and closed her eyes. She wouldn't panic. She wouldn't start sobbing. Yes, Kendrick was gone, but she had to look at the bright side of things.

She was completely free. Free of obligation. Free of her father. Free of her virginity. Free of her sappy, intact heart.

Yeah, that was shattered all over Kendrick's home. Every place he'd taken here. Every place he'd touched her. All the places he'd kissed her, commanded her, owned her… They all held parts of her heart.

Okay, the bright-side thinking wasn't working.

Now, it was time to leave. That seemed pretty clear since he'd snuck out on her, not even saying goodbye, not giving her a chance to beg for more. Obviously, he wanted to avoid a ugly situation. Of course, he did.

Fine. Time to go.

Fighting tears, Moriah headed back toward the bedroom. She dressed in a pair of peach-skin-soft jeans and a silky pink blouse. Beneath it, she couldn't resist wearing the blush-pink La Perla she loved so much when she'd explored

203

Kendrick's purchases yesterday. She'd never wear it again without remembering his face when she'd modeled it for him before church yesterday. Or how he'd bent her over the bench in the walk-in closet, almost making them late for the service.

Her body heated at the memory, a discordant contrast to the hollowness that filled her as she looked around his bedroom one last time. This was where she'd belonged to him. She didn't want to forget a detail. She pressed a hand to her chest. Pain radiated where her heart should be. Though she felt the beat there, it was of a ghost. She was leaving it behind when she stepped out the door.

Her eyes burned, but she refused to cry. Kendrick had given her exactly what she'd asked for. It had been a fantasy weekend, and nothing more was required of him.

A tiny voice inside her whispered that was a lie. Kendrick wouldn't lie to her. Kendrick wouldn't play with her emotions that way. She refused to acknowledge part of her consciousness. The proof was in his absence, wasn't it? Hope had no place in her life. Now, she had to be pragmatic and do what she must to take care of herself and her sister. She didn't need foolish love — oh, she loved Kendrick, even now when he'd disappointed her. She didn't know that she'd recover. No matter; she wouldn't have time for stupid emotions while she raised Jade.

This stolen weekend was over. Reality waited.

Tears streamed down her face as she headed toward the living room. Standing in the center, she looked around and realized she had no idea how she'd get home. She didn't have her purse, money or her phone, and therefore had no way to pay for a cab.

Great. Okay. She took a cleansing breath. She was resourceful. She'd figure this out. *Think, think, think—*

The sound of the door opening startled her.

"Oh good, you're up." Kendrick said. "I just got a call from—" He abruptly stopped speaking and set the tray and bag he was carrying on the counter. Appearing concerned, he rushed over to her. "Kitten, what's wrong? What happened?"

"Y-y-you were g-g-gone," she stammered, losing grip on her tightly held control now that he was here. "And I thought...I thought..."

He closed his arms around her and rested his cheek atop her head. "And you thought you couldn't trust me just like you haven't been able to trust anyone else in your life," he said quietly. It wasn't a question; there was no recrimination in his tone. "I should be angry that you can't trust me yet."

"I want to," she mumbled into his shirt, breathing his heady male scent and the light woodsy smell of his bodywash.

"We'll work on it. Moriah…" He leaned back slightly and lifted her chin with his fingers so she had to look at him. "I promise you that I will always tell you the truth, even when it's difficult—unless it's some happy surprise I've planned for you. I'm reserving that right."

She smiled at that. She suspected she looked like a watery hot mess.

"But," he continued and her heart stuttered, "one thing you should never ever doubt is that I love you with all I am and you're mine. I am never letting you go."

"That's more than one thing," she whispered, barely daring to tease him.

"It's all wrapped up together. Just like my whole world being wrapped up in you."

"I love you, too. I'm sorry I freaked out."

He nodded then brushed his mouth over hers, still holding her chin with his fingers. The kiss was all too brief before he straightened. "Come. Let's eat breakfast before we go deal with the unpleasantness, once and for all."

"Yay," she said dryly.

"Look at it as the doorway to the rest of our happy lives. One final flaming hoop to jump through."

"We'll probably have to go to court."

"Aren't you Suzy Sunshine this morning," he laughed, guiding her toward the kitchen island. "Yes, we might have to see him in court, but Jof won't be free to hurt you or steal from us anymore."

"You're right. I'm just nervous. Everything just seems so…" She shook her head, unable to explain how dread seemed to crush her from all sides as they readied for their confrontation with her father. She'd thought it was the fear of everything being over with Kendrick, but he was here with his reassurances and terror still loomed ahead of her, as if she was foolish to hope for the best because something horrible was yet to come. The only other time she'd felt this way was when her mother had died. She'd seemed to be making a rebound, stronger than been in months. But

Moriah had known. She'd woken that morning with this same oppressive, heavy cloud of trepidation over her. Her belly was full of tight knots and she couldn't take a deep breath.

She tried to convince herself she was overreacting, but nothing she told her self and none of Kendrick's reassurances calmed her.

Trying her best to act normal, Moriah pasted on a small smile and ate the donut and banana he'd brought her. She barely took more than a few sips of her coffee. The beloved beverage churned in her belly, the threat of vomiting all-to-real.

Kendrick glanced at his watch. "Ready?"

She shrugged. "Let's get this over with."

The elevator ride to the ground floor seemed too quick, and they walked through the building's lobby without anyone stopping them, even to say hello. Frank waited at the curb with Kendrick's town car. Of course, his bodyguard-driver-assistant-whatever would be coming along.

"Why didn't Frank come with you to the auction?" she asked, realizing for the first time that the man hadn't been there. It seemed odd to her now that Kendrick would have entered such a situation without him nearby.

208

"I wanted as few people as witnesses as possible. I didn't want him to…"

See her naked. Like everyone else there. Okay… "You're kind of a caveman about me."

"Get used to it. He *was* around though. He scooped out the place then waited on the plane—under protest. He was in the cockpit with the pilot during the trip."

"Ma'am. Sir," Frank greeted them as they approached and he opened the back door for them.

"Frank," Kendrick replied with a nod while she gave the bodyguard a small smile. She was too nervous for much more.

Once inside, Kendrick gave Frank directions then gathered her close to his side. "Relax. It's going to be okay," he assured her.

She had to get it together. She had to be strong, do what the cops said then take Jade out of there.

"I talked to Jenkins this morning," he said, pulling out his phone then dialing. "We're about twenty-five minutes out… Okay… No, we won't go in alone… Okay, right. Understood." He squeezed her shoulder, reassuring her. Hanging up, he turned to her. "The warrant's already been processed. They just need to arrest Jof. Cops are meeting us there. And a team from the FBI will be with them, as well as social services."

"Social Services?" she asked in distress.

"Because of Jade. Don't worry. Senator McKenzie's already smoothed things over for the transition. I spoke with her people this morning, too."

And she'd slept through that all. And when she'd woken, she'd thought he'd abandoned, yet all the while, he'd been working on her behalf.

As promised, the cops were at the end of the drive, out of sight from the house, when their car arrived. Frank pulled in then several cars followed.

"Stay outside," Kendrick told him.

"Boss, you remember I was Special Forces?" Frank argued.

"I remember I'm your boss, you took a near-fatal round to your thigh and I don't want you in there. I still don't agree with Moriah going in. I need you out here, ready to cover her if I send her running."

Though Kendrick didn't like it, the plan was for Moriah to let them into the house so there would no commotion to tip off Jofre and give him a chance to run or cause a problem. Then she'd stay in the foyer with him, out of the way while they led that fucker away in cuffs.

Jenkins and Jones hopped out of their plain blue vehicle and met them on the front stoop, while the woman from social services and four other officers waited on the walkway.

Silently, Moriah led the detectives into the mansion then held the door open for the other five law enforcement officers. Kendrick stayed close by her side. The house was silent, save for the ticking of the grandfather clock to the right side of the grandiose entryway. It made everything seem eerie, revving up Moriah's already overwrought nerves.

When a maid Moriah vaguely recognized came into the entryway, the woman's eyes went wide, but anything she would have said was forestalled by the shake if Moriah's head. Wisely, the servant disappeared in the direction from which she'd come — thankfully, the opposite way from Jof's home office.

A moment later, Mario, their butler hurried in, no doubt sent by the maid, and the officers reached for their weapons. The

211

manservant held his hands in front of him to show he wasn't a threat, and Moriah beckoned him closer.

"What's going on?" he asked.

"He's been embezzling. Millions. And…worse," she added, not wanting to reveal it all and pretty sure she wasn't allowed to do so anyway. "They're arresting him."

Mario appeared mildly surprised, but in his true butler fashion, he didn't display much emotion. She knew he did his job here but had never been much of a Jofre fan. He'd only stayed on because of loyalty to her mother.

"He's in his office?" she asked.

"Yes, Miss."

"And Jade?"

"She's at the library with her nanny. They're due back in a half hour."

"Thank you. And Mario," she said, before he turned away, "stay away from that wing of the house, and let the others know what's happening. The officers will be searching the house for evidence, so the staff needs to keep out of the way. In fact, you can send them home for now."

"Also, tell them I'll make sure you're all well taken care of," Kendrick said, squeezing her hand. She felt stronger with him beside her, though mostly she felt numb. She'd probably break down later, after Jade was asleep.

"Yes, Miss. Sir," Mario said with a small smile. Uncharacteristically, he patted her shoulder. "Your mother would be proud of you."

Then he disappeared, and she pointed the way to Jof's office. Looking around, this home seemed completely unfamiliar to her. Of course, she'd spent most of her formative and college years away at school, so she hadn't spent a ton of time here since she was a child. Jade would have a better life than she'd had, with no fears or worries because of her unpredictable parents.

"Are you ready?" Jenkins asked as he and Jones prepared to head into Jof's office while she stayed in the foyer. The four other officers stood off to the side, ready to follow. The woman from Social Services moved to wait Moriah and Kendrick. He rubbed Moriah's back, silently giving her his strength and support. It wasn't until then that she realized she was shaking.

"I'm ready," she whispered, praying everything went as planned and the feeling of dread knotting her stomach was nothing.

"You don't need to say anything to him," Jones said. We have everything we need, along with your statement on record, Mr. Bergana's statement and evidence, and our warrant. Once he's in custody, we'll begin our search for more."

"Okay." She didn't think she could speak coherently with her nerves choking her. Kendrick pulled her tight into his embrace, tipping his head over hers as if trying to shield her from what was happening.

"It's going to be all right," he murmured, rocking her slightly.

Moriah wrapped her arms around his waist, squeezing his and pressing her face into his chest as a commotion started down the hallway. Her father yelled, and she heard the deep, calm voices of the cops as they addressed him then announced their reason for the arrest. Then her father bellowed, and it sounded as if he were throwing things.

She closed her eyes. There was a louder thud then she heard Jenkins reading Jof's Miranda rights. It was almost over.

"I'll sue your asses off for this," Jof screamed as they led him toward the front of the house.

Suddenly Jof broke free, and dashed for the grandfather clock, reaching behind it and pulling out a revolver. He spun and aimed at her.

"No," Kendrick yelled. He shoved her behind her as shots fired then he was falling. Everything moved into slow motion as her pulse roared past her ears. She collapsed to her knees beside her lover, horrified by the blood covering his chest, the stain spreading. Vaguely aware of her father being tackled, of the chandelier shattering with another shot, she pressed her hands to Kendrick's chest sobbing.

"No," she screamed. "No!"

Kendrick weakly lifted his hand and touched her face as she bent over him. "It'll be all right," he whispered. "Be all right."

Then his eyes closed, and her scream turned to sorrowful wails.

Chapter Eighteen

Kendrick lay still beneath Moriah's hands as she kept them pressed to his wound. She couldn't see through her tears.

"Ma'am, let me take over." Frank knelt beside her and nudged aside her bloody hands. The guard looked torn apart, probably because he'd been forced to wait outside instead of being in here.

"He can't die, Frank. He can't…" A sob cut off her words.

Warm, feminine hands circled her shoulders, and the woman from Social Services guided Moriah to her feet. Two of the police officers dropped down next to Frank to help him.

"Paramedics will be here in a couple minutes," the woman said. Though her words were calm, they trembled slightly. Gently, she edged Moriah toward the door.

"I can't leave him!" Moriah protested. "I can't...I... I promised to stay with him."

"We're not leaving. We're just giving them space. I'm Nancy, by the way. I'll stay right here with you."

"Ma'am," Mario said. Moriah blinked at him because she knew he hadn't been there moments ago. She didn't think he had anyway. Ever efficient, he handed her a damp cloth while he held a second one and a towel. When she didn't move to clean up, he said, "Miss Jade will be back soon."

Right. And her sister couldn't be covered in blood. "I need to take care of here, but I can't leave Kendrick," she murmured, torn. Her eyes didn't leave him for even a second as the three men leaned over him. Blindly, she wiped at her hands with the cloth. She didn't even look when Mario took it from her. He grasped her arm and ran the other cloth over it.

"She has a nanny, correct?" Nancy asked.

"Yes," Moriah answered numbly.

"We'll take care of your sister," Mario assured her.

"And...I'll explain that her father is going away and that she will be in your care," Nancy added. "With details appropriate for her age, of course. There's no need to tell her exactly what's going on."

"Thank you," Moriah said. She could barely think beyond knowing the man she loved lay on the floor bleeding out from being shot by her father—a shot aimed for *her!*

"Moriah," Kendrick murmured. His eyes were closed and she wasn't even sure if he was fully conscious.

"I'm here," she said, moving closer.

"O-okay?" he asked.

"I'm fine. You protected me. My father's been cuffed and taken out of here."

"Should have already been god-damned cuffed," Jones grumbled.

Moriah ignored him, though she figured she'd get answers later. Her father could be smooth. He'd probably asked them to preserve what little dignity he had left and to cuff him at

219

the car rather than parade him past the staff while bound.

"I'll...always protect...you," Kendrick told her.

"I know," she sobbed. "I know. Just...don't... Just get better!"

"Never leaving you, kitten."

Before she could reply, the EMTs rushed in and Kendrick passed out again. And he did leave her, because she wasn't allowed to go with him. Because of his injuries, he was being transported via helicopter and only Frank was allowed to go.

Agony crushed down on her. Moriah couldn't help but fear she'd never see Kendrick again, that he'd die before she was allowed at his side again.

* * * *

"I'm sorry, but you can't go up. Only family or those on his approved list are allowed," the nurse told Moriah.

"I'm not on his list? Moriah Cabraro?" Moriah repeated. Frank didn't make sure she could get in? "I have my ID if you need it."

"No. I'm sorry. I—"

The rest of her words were lost on Moriah as she backed away, her thoughts whirling. Frank had gone with Kendrick when he'd been airlifted while she'd gathered her purse, phone and car keys then driven to the hospital, leaving the police to comb over the house, with directions to Mario to help in any way they needed. Nancy, the social worker, was meeting Jade. Beyond her sister, Mariah's only thought was in getting to Kendrick. And now...she couldn't.

Feeling lost, she pushed her hand into her hair and looked around. She could sit in the waiting room until...

Until what? Until Kendrick remembered her? Or Frank? Or... God, what if he died. She could be sitting there waiting while he was... dead. Moriah choked on the thought, her chest going so tight with pain and panic she feared she might pass out.

She stepped back up to the desk. She had to ask. She had to... "He's alive though?"

The attendant's eyes filled with sympathy. "I'm sorry but I can't give out any patient information."

Right. Privacy laws.

Moriah nodded, not feeling any better. She didn't know what to do.

221

"If you want to leave your contact information, I can make sure it's delivered to his people."

Moriah nodded again and took the paper and pen the woman offered then quickly wrote her first name and call phone number. After she'd handed it over, she left the hospital to go home to Jade. Her sister was supposed to be her main focus, her purpose in all this. She couldn't lose sight of that.

She'd wait until Frank had her information and got this cleared up so she could see Kendrick. She'd take care of Jade and wait for Kendrick to call.

* * * *

He didn't call. Frank didn't call. And as the long days passed, Moriah grew surer that she'd been forgotten. Well, perhaps forgotten wasn't the right word. More like pushed aside like an inconvenience one wished they could forget. She wouldn't have thought that of Kendrick, but as the days stretched into three weeks, it became clear that despite his promises, he'd changed his mind. Perhaps, getting shot because of her had made that decision for him. Just in case, she'd tried to call him at the hospital a few times but hadn't made it past the switchboard. Apparently, being a high-profile patient kept unapproved callers from getting through. She wasn't approved.

Her bank account hold had been cleared, so she now had access to her cash. It felt like dirty money, but until she was settled with Jade and found employment, she had little choice other than to use it. She'd earned it, hadn't she?

Moriah bit hard into her cheek, refusing to cry again. She took a deep breath and glanced over at her sister. They were mid-flight to Orlando where Moriah intended to take Jade to all the attractions. To the little girl who'd never really been anywhere, it was the trip of her young life. Right now, Jade had in headphones while she watched a movie on her tablet. Moriah, in the aisle seat, stared blindly over her at the clouds outside the small window. Silently, she vowed they'd have an adventure together while Moriah got her shit together. Meanwhile, the mansion was being closed down. It couldn't be sold until Jof was in prison, but she'd seen to removing all of her and Jade's things, storing them until she decided where they'd live.

She hadn't felt an ounce of guilt when she'd cleared the cash from her father's safe — the police had only wanted the files hidden in there. From the stash, she'd given the staff generous severance packages. Mario would oversee them through today, then everyone would be gone.

And now, she and Jade were essentially homeless. It was an odd feeling, having no real address, no place to call home. They were two people with no roots, no place to have mail delivered.

After their two weeks in Florida, Moriah would take care of that. She might not have her college degree yet, having another year to go, but she had experience, smarts and enough cash to see them through for a long while. She'd find them a small home, have their things delivered from storage and go from there.

An overhead announcement came on to tell them they were about to land, and Moriah nudged Jade. "We're going to land. You need to shut down your movie."

"Aw!" Jade protested.

Moriah clicked her tongue and gave a half shrug. "It's the rules. You can watch it again once we get to the rental car, okay, sweetness."

Jade gave a dramatic sigh. "Okay. Can we have McDonalds? I'm hungry."

"Maybe. Or maybe..." She hadn't told Jade where they were headed. "Maybe we can see what Disney has to eat."

"Disney?" the little girl asked in hushed awe.

"Yes. We're staying right there and doing all the things."

Jade sucked in a breath, shaking in her excitement. "Moriah, you are the bestest sister in the *whole* world! Really? We're going to see the princesses and Mickey?"

"Really."

The little girl was practically jumping though belted into her seat. And the first joy Moriah had felt in weeks, slide through her, lightening the stone that had taken up residence in her gut. This was good. Coming here with Jade was the best decision she could make.

She held Jade's hand as they landed, knowing everything was worth it. Jade had been her core reason. Knowing she was safe and happy was the world to Moriah, and her own personal drama faded—at least for now. She didn't fool herself into believing it wouldn't slam into her full force when she lay in bed tonight.

With Jade practically bouncing beside her the whole time—sometimes *actually* bouncing— Moriah gathered their luggage and picked up her rental car. She hadn't lied when she'd told Kendrick she could drive. In fact, she was a great

225

driver, something that came in handy in the Orlando traffic.

Jade talked a mile a minute and before Moriah knew it, they'd gotten to the resort and checked in. Her sister was still a ball of vibrating energy once they got to their suite, while Moriah sank bonelessly onto the couch. Jade would likely run her into the ground this week. Already mentally exhausted, Moriah would be physically exhausted, too. Probably not a terrible thing. Sleeping like the dead would keep her mind off Kendrick.

"Hey, Jade Bug," she wheedled. "How about you go check out your room and give me a few minutes to check my messages, okay?"

"Than can we go see Mickey and Ariel?"

"We can try. I'm not sure we'll find them, but we'll have some fun. *And find some yummy food,*" she said, adding extra emphasis to the last.

"Good. I'm *starving,*" Jade replied with the over-drama of a typical six-year-old.

Moriah grinned. "Give me a few minutes then we can go wander."

"Okay, Rye-rye."

Jade skipped off while Moriah reached for her phone. It was still shut off from the flight, so she waited what seemed an eternity for it to boot up. It started ringing immediately with a number she didn't know. Her brow scrunched as she looked at it, but before she decided to answer, the call went to voicemail.

Suddenly, notifications of missed calls and texts started popping up. The phone started ringing again. The same number. It was from her home area code, so taking a deep breath, she answered.

"Hello?" she said cautiously.

"Where the fuck are you?"

"Kendrick?" she breathed. Despite his harsh greeting, her heart soared at his voice.

"Moriah," he growled in warning. "Where are you?"

His tone pulled her from her shock and surprising anger leapt up in its place. "Where are *you*?"

"Trying to find you."

"Funny, no one's bothered to call me or send me any messages in the past three weeks. When the hospital wouldn't let me in, I give them

227

my information for your people. Nothing. Way to show me how much I matter as I sat worrying myself sick over you, wondering if you were dead or alive. It's okay though—"

"Moriah—"

"No, really, it's okay. I get it. It was just a…fling, I guess. You were saying all the right things to make me comfortable. Flings shouldn't expect hospital-room access. It's not like I was actually your fiancée or something."

"No! I—"

"It's *fine*. I get it. I'm fine. Apparently, you're fine—and I'm happy for that. Now, it's time to move on. Thanks for the memories."

"No, it's—"

"Rye, my stomach's growly. I wanna go see Mickey," Jade said from a few feet away. Moriah held up a finger for her to wait a second.

"I have to go," she told Kendrick. "I'm glad you're well. I—"

"No—"

"'Bye, Kendrick."

"Moriah, don't you hang—" he was yelling as she disconnected.

Standing, she powered off the phone then tossed it on the couch before holding out her hand to her sister. Inside, she was broken. Kendrick sounded great. Absolutely fucking perfect, and here, she'd been losing her mind over how bad the shot must have been. But when nothing had been reported on the news, she'd known. Hearing him so hale and demanding drove that point home.

She just wasn't that important to him.

Where the fuck are you?

Kendrick's tone had made it clear he obviously expected a relationship of convenience with her, for her to wait around to answer his beck and call. *Pfft.* Nope. She didn't have time for his games—not with Jade to care for. Kendrick couldn't even bother to have his people contact her to let her know he was okay or better yet, call her himself to let her know he was thinking of her, that he wanted her to come see him in the hospital, that he missed her...or that he loved her. For three weeks, she'd been so sure he didn't want her anymore. And when she'd *finally* come to terms with that heartbreaking fact, he had the nerve to call her.

"Come on, you," she beckoned Jade, deciding here and now to move on. "Let's go have lunch then find some fun."

"Yay!" Jade squealed, resuming her exuberant jumping. "I wanna be a princess!"

Moriah smiled. "Don't we all."

Chapter Nineteen

Teacups — check. Small World — check. Princess-bejeweled mouse ears — check. One super-tired little girl — check.

Moriah carried Jade down the hallway to their suite, glad her sister was fairly small for a six-year-old. Over the other shoulder, she had a tote filled with their treasures from the day. Trying not to wake Jade, she wrestled her keycard from her pocket then unlocked her front door. To her surprise, the lights were on as she entered. The surprise gave way to knee-buckling shock as she saw the tall figure waiting for her a few feet away. A small scream escaped as she took a few steps backward. He was already coming toward her when she realized who it was a split-second later.

"What are you doing here?" she demanded.

"Waiting for you, obviously." He reached for Jade, but Moriah turned slightly to deflect him. "I'm not going to hurt her," he growled.

She shook her head, stepping around him. She let the tote bag slide to the floor then headed toward Jade's room. "Correct me if I'm wrong," she said, "but didn't you get shot recently. You don't need to rip something open."

"She's not that heavy, and I've done nothing but heal for three weeks."

Moriah scowled at the reminder. "Right. And remind me, what are you doing here?"

"Coming to get my woman."

"Really? She's in Florida somewhere?" she scoffed. Without waiting for an answer, she placed Jade on her bed.

"Don't be a smartass," he whisper-yelled from the doorway while she took off her sister's shoes then tucked her into bed. Optimally, she should be putting her into jammies but dealing with Kendrick ranked higher at the moment.

She glared at him, then skirted around him again to leave the room. He closed the door behind them then stalked after her. He was inches away when she turned to face him. "What are you doing *here?*" she demanded, this time indicating the room.

"When I heard Jade say she wanted to see Mickey, I figured out where you were—well, generally anyway. I narrowed my options down to Florida or California...or maybe a Disney cruise. It didn't take my people long to find your flight info and where you were staying, once I knew you'd left town."

Handy. He'd told her he had hackers-but-not-hackers he could rely on. "That doesn't answer my question. Maybe I should ask *why* are you here?"

He huffed an annoyed sigh and caught her hand, not letting go when she tried to pull away. And it took all her effort to do even that since all her nerve endings were jumping gleefully at the touch. She couldn't deny she wanted him. Nothing about her attraction to him had dimmed. But he'd hurt her heart—she couldn't forget that.

Kendrick sat on the couch where she'd tossed her phone earlier. As he pulled her onto his lap, she noticed it was now carefully placed on the coffee table. Not wanting to be so close to him, she tried to shift away but his steely embrace kept her right where he wanted her, flush against his chest. Mindful that he'd been hurt and not wanting to reinjure him, she didn't fight as hard to get away as she might have in other circumstances.

"I never got your information," he said, once she'd settled, albeit stiffly, on his lap. "I was in the hospital for almost the entire three weeks, longer than necessary, I'm sure, because they didn't want the liability of something going wrong with a high-profile patient."

"I left my number with the desk."

"Never got it. Frank never got it, either. I swear...this past week I've been talking about getting you fitted with some kind of tracking device—"

"You're not chipping me like a dog or something."

"I was thinking of it being in a bracelet or your engagement ring or something."

"I think you're getting ahead of yourself; don't you?" At his frustration over not being able to find her, her anger was lessening, but not enough that she was ready to talk about the future he alluded to.

"No. If you haven't realized I'm never giving you up, then you're the one behind in the story."

"Right," she scoffed. "It took your hackers mere hours to find me in another state, but you couldn't track me down in the same city?"

"Frank got you put on my list right away, but you never showed. They had me drugged up, and in that state, I thought you didn't want to see me. Then we couldn't find you. It's true that once I was more coherent for longer periods, we had to deal with the fallout from your father's arrest and the embezzling from *Berg Trade*. Still, my mind was never far from you, even when I was getting rid of most of the board—I'd been poised to do that anyway, but there was red tape. The number I had for you was wrong—old, I guess. Your message still played, so apparently, the number wasn't deactivated. I thought you were ignoring me. Today when I got out of the hospital, I went directly to your house and demanded Mario let me speak to you."

"My father gave me a new phone with a new number last year. I was getting weird calls from overseas…"

He stared at her as they both realized those calls had likely been trafficking contacts. Moriah pressed a hand to her stomach as her dinner roiled. Kendrick held her tighter, and she pressed her face into his neck.

"That's when I found out you had a different number than the one I'd been given. I was furious, you know? That you'd ignore me like that? I was itching to take you over my knee and remind you who you belong to."

"I thought you didn't want me," she whispered, inhaling his scent now that her anger was dissipating and she realized it was all a big misunderstanding with multiple hurdles to navigate. "I left my number at the hospital and asked that someone call me when it was okay to come see you. No one called."

"Kitten, I promise you, no one delivered that message."

She squeezed her arms around his shoulders. "I was so scared for you then so sad that you didn't want me."

"I'll always want you. Moriah, I'm never letting you get away from me. When Mario said you'd left town...I just about lost my mind," he confessed. "He said you put all the things you wanted in storage and that he didn't know where you'd gone with Jade."

That was true. Not wanting to burden the man who was already overburdened in this whole situation, I'd only told him I was taking Jade on vacation and would check in with him to see how things were going.

"Thank God he had your correct number," Kendrick added.

"I'm glad," she confessed. "How did you get in here, though?"

"Billionaire magic."

"Mm-hmm," she grumbled. "Well, we're planning to be here for two weeks."

"I know. I, too, am planning to be here for two weeks."

"You're going to work from here?"

He shrugged. "A little. Mostly not."

She grinned. "Does that mean you're up to all that is the Magic Kingdom?"

"I'll even wear the mouse ears."

"Jade will insist." She smoothed her hands down his chest, remembering the last time she'd had her hands on him here. She'd been covering the bullet wound in his chest. Her palm made a circle over the general area. "They wouldn't tell me anything at the hospital. What... I mean..."

She closed her eyes. "I know you were shot but—
"

His hand covered hers and he guided her fingers. "Bullet went in here. Nicked a rib but mostly went clean into the lung. That was the tricky part of everything. They sent me straight to surgery and I've been recovering since. Have another week before the doctor feels I'll be back to tip-top—well, close to it anyway. Could actually be a couple more weeks, but I've always been a quick healer."

"Thank you for not trying to be all macho and tough about it."

"That would just make it take longer before I'm back to one-hundred percent for my girl." He caught her chin and brushed his lips over hers, and Moriah swore the zing went clear to her core. "I love you, Moriah."

Her breath caught on a jagged inhale. "I...I love you."

Tears filled her eyes as he leaned his forehead into hers. She was back in his arms, back in the embrace of her forever.

His thumb brushed back and forth where he still held her chin. "You should know...you're getting a spanking for hanging up on me then turning off your phone."

238

That sent another thrill through her. God help her, she'd kind of come to love that. It always turned out well for her. "I don't know," she teased. "Do you think you're up for it? I wouldn't want you to hurt yourself."

"Oh, I'm very up for it. I'm plenty well enough to take you in hand, little kitten. Besides…you're going to be a very good girl and not fight me." He guided her to her feet then stood. "Now, show me to your room."

She wasn't so sure how she felt about his assertion about her behavior, but she threaded her fingers through his anyway, then led him into her portion of the suite. It took her about three seconds to realize he hadn't needed her to show him the way since his suitcase stood beside hers.

Moriah raised a brow at him, but Kendrick looked wholly unrepentant. "I know where I'm supposed to be," he said. "More so, I know where you're supposed to be."

"Oh? And where's that?"

"In my arms. Every night. You and Jade *are* moving in with me after this vacation."

"I…"

"It's not a question. It's happening. I've already arranged for your things to be delivered

239

to the penthouse. They'll be there when we arrive, and Jade's room will be all set up for her."

"You're a little high-handed, you know."

"What I know is that you're mine, and I'm taking care of you." He flipped the lock on the door then closed the space between them. Immediately, he lifted the hem of the Mickey Mouse T-shirt she wore. Dropping it to their feet, he reached for the button of her denim shorts. She kicked off her sandals just before she slid the pants down her legs, leaving her in just her bra and panties.

She shifted her weight, her tongue darting along her bottom lip as she surveyed him, fully clothed in jeans and a Henley, the sleeves pushed up his muscular arms. While she watched, captivated by him and realizing she'd missed him even more than she'd realized, he moved around her and sat on the edge of the bed. Like a flower following the sun, she pivoted to face him. Never breaking their gaze, he slowly nodded once and patted his thigh.

"Are you serious?" she asked.

"Completely."

She huffed and crossed her arms over her chest.

"Moriah, where are we?" he asked evenly.

"My hotel room."

He raised an eyebrow. She sighed, seeing exactly where this was going.

"The bedroom of my hotel suite," she amended.

"And what does that mean?"

She looked away. "You're being unreasonable."

"And?" he asked, not missing a beat.

"And you think you're in charge."

"I think?"

She didn't say anything, and he let the silence stretch, neither of them moving, neither of them willing to concede. Moriah knew she would. She'd promised, and damn it, she wanted to. Every part of her was drawn to him and his damn dominating rules. She could also see his point, even though she didn't want to admit it. In her pique of anger, she'd blocked the opportunity to fix the situation between them — not that she was taking responsibility for the misunderstanding that had led to three weeks of misery.

241

"It's not my fault we've been apart for three weeks," she finally said, making sure they were on the same page about that.

"No, it's not. The only issue at discussion is the phone call and you hanging up on me — and not telling me where you were when I asked."

She rolled her eyes, still not looking at him while she fiddled with her ear. "Bellowed you mean."

"Moriah." There was no missing the warning in his tone.

She glared at him. "I'm not a child."

"Clearly." His eyes roamed up and down her body. Leaning forward, he rested his arms on his legs, then winced and adjusted so one arm bore no weight. "I thought we worked this all out before. You're disobedient; I spank you. It's the game we play. Our dynamic."

"That was weeks ago," she said.

"Your tastes have changed since then? Mine haven't."

No, hers hadn't either. She was just being difficult, and they both knew it.

Sitting up straighter, he held out his hand. His stare brooked no further argument. Silently, Moriah placed her hand in his and let him pull her toward him until she stood between his parted legs. Her arms looped around his shoulders as she looked down at him, though they were nearly eye to eye.

"Is it always going to be a fight?" he asked.

"Probably," she replied.

He shook his head with a half-smile.

"You like it," she added.

Kendrick made a noncommittal sound and pulled her closer, so she tumbled against him, and he fell backward onto the bed with her clasped tight to him.

"I shouldn't be lying on your chest," she exclaimed, trying to wiggle away.

"You're fine. Stay still. Just let me hold you for a minute." He pressed his face into her neck. "God, I've missed this. I've missed you so much. You have no idea."

"If it was anything like I missed you, I have some idea. It sucked being away from you. Thinking you didn't want me…"

243

His arms tightened. "Never think that. I will always want you—"

"You can't know that. Things change."

"No, not this. This love we have between us? That's not changing. Can't you feel it? Deep down? How real it is? I've never felt this way about anyone or anything else."

She had to admit she did. Deep down, she knew she'd never fall out of love with Kendrick. Even if something happened and they ended us apart, she'd always love him.

"Yes," she admitted, resting her head on his chest and listening to his heartbeat. It was so solid and strong, telling her that he really was well-recovered from being shot, though she didn't doubt he had a way to go before being one-hundred percent again, regardless of how he might try to convince her otherwise. She started to pull free of his embrace, but he tightened his hold—nothing wrong with his arm muscles!

"Where are you going?" he complained.

"Not far. Let me up." She sat up and straddled him when he relaxed his hold. "I want to see."

Kendrick groaned. "No, you don't. Besides…" He guided her hand to where the bullet had hit him. "There's a bandage over it still."

She gently ran her fingers over the spot. A few inches left and it would have hit his heart. She swallowed hard.

He grasped the hand and brought it to his lips. "Baby, I'm okay."

"But—"

"No buts. No what ifs. We're both all right."

"I hate that this happened to you."

He grimaced. "I'm glad it was me and not you."

"Better if it was neither." Her fingers went to the hem of his Henley, intent on her mission.

"Moot point," he replied. Shifting her to sit beside him, he sat upright and pulled off his shirt. He stood then removed his pants, leaving him in just his black boxer-briefs. The bulge from his need was evident and she licked her lips, hoping she could taste it tonight. "Okay, enough delaying," he said, sitting then patting his thigh again.

Moriah huffed. "Really."

"Let's not start that loop again."

"Fine."

She stood then maneuvered herself over his parted legs. Kendrick smoothed his hand along her back. His fingertips trailed along her spine, lifting goose bumps and making her shiver at the sensual caress. Now that she was in position, he seemed to be in no big hurry to do more than touch her and she relaxed. Her anticipation grew with each featherlight drag along her skin until she was literally trembling with her need for him to get to the spanking. Her panties were damp from her need of him — something she wasn't even sure she'd get — and she wondered if he'd push them down to expose her ass for his palm.

As if knowing her thought, he slipped his hand inside her panties to curve around one ass cheek and squeeze. Moriah couldn't contain her moan. He inched the lacy garment down her thighs until it was around her knees. She shivered as he dragged his fingertips up along her thigh then traced the lower curve of her ass.

"You're torturing me," she complained.

"But does it feel good?"

She groaned, pressing her face into his leg.

"Do you know why you're in this position?" he asked.

"Because you're a sadist."

He chuckled darkly. "Try again, bad girl."

"It's not my fault a misunderstanding kept us apart."

"No, it's not."

"I shouldn't have hung up on you."

"No, you shouldn't have."

"And...I should have listened."

"Right."

"And you really like to spank me, so it works into your evil plan. Because really, you're not one to hit me in anger."

"I never would." He kept caressing her, touching her all over — except where she really wanted him — so when the first blow of his hand on her ass came, she was wholly unprepared. Moriah reared up, crying out then moaning.

"Yes," she whispered as his free arm clamped over her upper back, holding her down. She whimpered at the heat spreading along her rear as the spanks rained down — the heat and the moisture that was quickly dampening her pussy and slicking her upper thighs. God help her, but she loved it when he did this. She might call him a weirdo, but she was right there with him, wanting exactly what he was giving.

"Kendrick," she gasped out. "Oh...*God!*" Colors cascaded around her as the last few strikes to her ass plunged her over the edge and into a soaring orgasm. Kendrick was moving her and filling her with her bent over the bed. Her climax expanded, rolling over her in stronger waves as he pummeled into her from behind, fucking her hard and with all the frustration they'd both experienced the past few weeks.

"Fuck, kitten," he muttered. "Fuck yes. You feel...*so good*...squeezing me so hard with that pussy. You're mine, Moriah. Mine."

"Yes," she promised.

"You like my cock taking you like this, don't you? Claiming you. Owning you."

"More. I want more. Harder," she begged, even though she wasn't sure he could go harder without breaking her. She'd missed him so much, needed him so badly, that nothing seemed enough in this moment. It might be a long time before either of them were sated enough to calm.

He leaned over her and kissed her shoulder. Rather than going harder, his pumps slowed, each pull and drove dragging over every part of her sensitive, inner walls, so intimate and caring. His lips moved along her neck up to just behind her ear.

"I love you. You're my everything," he murmured. "I'm nothing without you. You make me whole. You give me purpose. Don't ever leave me."

"Never," she vowed. "I love you. I love you."

"Good because I'm never letting you go."

She belonged. Not to him, but here in his embrace. He may have paid cash to save her in that auction, but the real payment had been giving her his heart. He owned her, and she owned him just as much, having paid with her heart, too. And knowing that calmed every storm inside her. With him, she was safe in a way she never had been.

Moriah, reached back, cupping his head and holding him to her as he continued making love to her and kissing her neck and shoulders. "I'm never letting you go, either. Ever. This is where our forever begins."

Kendrick pushed deep one last time, his forehead against the nape of her neck, and stilled, other than involuntary shudders as he lost himself in her.

"Forever," he promised. "Forever."

Epilogue

Jade splashed in the pool while Moriah lay on one of the loungers beside it.

"She looks happy."

Moriah glanced over at Kendrick. Lounging on the chair pushed right up against hers, he wore a black swimsuit and a white tee. They'd been back at his penthouse for a week now, after their two weeks at Disney. All three of them were settling into their new life together, made easier by a few of her father's former staff coming to work for them. None had been complicit in his crimes, and Moriah felt comfortable with Mario running their household and Jade's nanny, Anna, taking care of the little girl. Moriah had brought on the cook who'd practically raised her, as well.

"She is happy," she said. She smiled at him. "So am I."

"You better be."

She giggled. "Or what, Mr. Bergana? I'm feeling pretty safe from a spanking right now."

"Don't you think I don't have my ways. I do." He brought her left hand to his lips. "Besides, Mrs. Bergana, if you weren't happy, I do whatever was necessary to change that. Anything for my wife."

Oh yeah, there was that. The trip home from the Magic Kingdom had included a detour to Las Vegas. Neither of them had family, other than Jade who was with them. Frank had been there as well, having been their shadow all through their vacation. He'd stood up as their witness at the little chapel they'd chosen.

Jade had been shy for about three point two seconds when she'd met Kendrick the morning after their reunion then immediately started pestering him about coming with her to see Mickey. Moriah had soon learned he was a sucker to the little girl. For a time, she'd worried about how spoiled her sister — and any future children — might be. Then when Jade had thrown a tantrum over wanting to stay longer at the park one night, she'd witness Kendrick jumping into action and shutting down the behavior in a firm voice. His boundaries were wide but he'd been clear about his expectations. Seeing it had reassured Moriah that he could hack the dad thing, though they'd both be tried.

She stroked her fingers along the top of his hand. "So I was thinking…"

"That's dangerous."

"Jade has her music lessons this afternoon. Frank and Anna can take her to it. Maybe we could…find something to do together."

"Something in our bedroom, perhaps?"

"Well…" she reached into the pocket of her coverup and produced two pretty clamps that looked like flat flowers with an opening in the center of each for a nipple. "I thought maybe you'd like to try these. Maybe while we use the cuffs that I found in the bedside table."

"My naughty kitten."

"You love it."

"With everything in me." Kendrick stood and reached for her hand. "Frank," he called as he pulled her to her feet. "Moriah and I need to see to some business. Make sure Jade gets to her piano lesson…and maybe some ice cream afterward."

"Yes!" Jade cheered before cannonballing into the water.

"Yes, sir," Frank said with a laugh, shaking off water.

Then Kendrick was pulling Moriah inside and toward their bedroom while she laughed, loving this man and everything her life had become.

About the Authors

~ Tia Fanning ~

Tia Fanning has discovered that she always writes a little of herself in every story, and in that vulnerability, is committed to writing the best stories she can, challenging herself and her readers to experience the full range of emotions in every adventure presented. Be it love, lust, humor, grief, or even pushing cultural boundaries that might be deemed shocking (or very uncomfortable) by many mainstream readers, Tia believes it is her responsibility as an author to tell the story as honestly as possible without letting her fears, societal pressure, or the possibility of censorship shackle her creativity. Life is a spontaneous, thrilling journey filled with highs and lows and unexpected twists and turns, and Tia wants her stories to reflect that awesome reality.

* * * *

~ Brynn Paulin ~

When it comes to books and movies, Brynn Paulin has one rule: there must be a happy ending. After that one requirement, anything else goes. And it just might in any of her books.

Brynn lives in Michigan, where she likes to spoil her children and dogs — not necessarily in that order. She also loves to cook, travel and spend far too much time on social media. Brynn conducts workshops at writers' conferences around the country as she enjoys mentoring and meeting new people.

According to Brynn, her writing success can be attributed to an eclectic collection of music, her local road construction crews, a trusty notebook, and of course, the people in her life who've finally accepted that everything is research — or will be.

You can fine Brynn at www.brynnpaulin.com.

www.ingramcontent.com/pod-product-compliance
Lightning Source LLC
Chambersburg PA
CBHW061955170626
46813CB00006B/2646